Viscount
and the
Vicar's
DAUGHTER

A Victorian Romance

MIMI MATTHEWS

THE VISCOUNT AND THE VICAR'S DAUGHTER
A Victorian Romance
Copyright © 2018 by Mimi Matthews

E-Book: 978-0-9990364-2-6
Paperback: 978-0-9990364-3-3

Cover Image: George P. A. Healy (1813–1894). Euphemia White Van Rensselaer. 1842. Oil on canvas, 115.1 x 89.2 cm. Bequest of Cornelia Cruger, 1923. Metropolitan Museum of Art.

Dedication

For Ash and Sapphie

Chapter One

North Yorkshire, England
Autumn, 1861

ristan Sinclair, Viscount St. Ashton, strode through the woods that bordered the ramshackle estate of his hosts, Lord and Lady Fairford. His father, the Earl of Lynden, was waiting for him back at the house. To beard him in his proverbial den, no doubt. Why else would he have tracked him to the wilds of Yorkshire, seeking him out at one of the most notorious house parties of the season?

"Your father is here, my lord," his groom had whispered as Tristan dismounted from his horse and tossed him the reins. "He is taking tea with Lady Fairford and has asked to be informed the moment you arrive."

Tristan was tired and irritable. He'd spent all day in the saddle. His servants had travelled ahead in the carriage, leaving the posting inn at the crack of dawn, while he'd remained abed, sleeping off the effects of a night of heavy drinking. And now, here he was, hiding out in the woods as if he were a boy of ten instead of a man of two and thirty.

He struck a low-hanging branch with his riding whip, severing the wet leaves with a loud, satisfying crunch. "Damn and blast!"

And then he heard it.

The unmistakable sound of a woman weeping in the woods.

Tristan stopped where he stood and listened. Yes. It was, indeed, a woman. He would recognize that muffled sound anywhere. He'd certainly heard it enough in his lifetime. More often than not, he'd been the cause of it. And yet… this weeping woman did not sound at all like the distraught mistresses, angry actresses, and spoiled heiresses he'd often provoked to tears.

This woman sounded as if her heart was breaking.

It seemed to be coming from within a cluster of trees just up ahead. There had been a broken down little folly there once, a popular location for lovers' trysts, as well as the many and varied debaucheries that were the hallmark of Lord and Lady Fairford's house parties. He'd once met a raven-haired widow there in the moonlight. Meg something? Or was it Mary? He couldn't recall. It had been years ago when such anonymous, amorous adventures still held some appeal for him.

Perhaps that was what he was hearing now? A liaison gone wrong? It wouldn't be unthinkable that a gentleman might bring his lover here to break things off with her. That would certainly explain the tears.

He would do better to ignore it and continue on his way. A random weeping woman was none of his affair.

Unless she was hurt.

Tristan was far less compassionate toward women than he'd been in his youth. He'd spent too many seasons being pursued by marriage-minded mamas and young ladies determined to wed the heir to one of the wealthiest earldoms in the country. For years he'd avoided the canniest tricks and the most outlandish traps, all the while becoming more and more jaded about the female sex.

Nevertheless, something about that pitiful sound compelled him forward.

He was vaguely conscious of the state of his appearance. His greatcoat and breeches were stained from travel. His cravat was a wilted disgrace and his boots, normally polished to a mirror-shine, were scuffed and filthy. Good God, but he must look like some shabby country squire! And, as if that image were not repulsive enough, he was well aware that he reeked of horses, sweat, and the aftereffects of a night of heavily liquored self-pity.

Not that any of that had ever mattered to a woman before.

Tristan came to a gap in the trees and, turning his large frame sideways, ducked through it. Wet leaves brushed his greatcoat, the smell of damp wood and sodden grass permeating the air. His eyes found the folly at the edge of the small clearing, exactly as he remembered it. Like much on the Fairfords' estate, it was in desperate need of repair. Half the roof had rotted away and the steps leading up to it were splintered and broken.

There inside, he saw the small, hunched figure of a woman in a drab, ill-fitting gown. A ray of sunlight through the branches of the trees glinted and sparkled off of something on her face.

Spectacles.

Tristan grimaced. He didn't need to go any closer to identify one of the ranks of colorless, bespectacled lady's companions who trailed meekly in the wake of Lady Hortensia Brightwell. Every year, Lady Brightwell had a new one. And yet, somehow, they always looked the same. Hair scraped back into a tight little knot. Shapeless, drooping gowns. And, on every single one of them, spectacles.

He'd long suspected that Lady Brightwell chose her companions specifically for their lack of charm and beauty.

Tristan hesitated only a moment before striding forward to the folly. He had no interest in comforting a dreary little spinster, but if the alternative was returning to the house where his father was waiting to read him a lecture, comfort her he would. And who better? If there was one thing the Viscount St. Ashton understood, it was women.

"I beg your pardon, ma'am," he said as he vaulted up the broken steps.

At the sound of his deep voice, the woman sprang up from her seat. A crumpled paper fell from her lap onto the ground. She looked at it and then looked up at him. For an instant, Tristan thought she might bolt.

He raised a staying hand. "Don't be uneasy," he said. "I mean you no harm. Indeed, I meant to offer you some assistance."

She stared at him through spectacles that were steamed from her tears and then, with a choking sigh, she sank back onto the wooden bench and covered her face with her hands.

A rare pang of sympathy briefly softened his expression. The poor little antidote. One might think that she had just discovered that her entire world had come to an end. Perhaps she had been given the sack? Or perhaps one of Lady Fairford's less reputable houseguests had attempted to steal a kiss?

Moving as carefully as he would if he were approaching a wild animal, Tristan crossed the folly to stand at her side. He did not wait for an invitation. This was not a drawing room in Mayfair and she was not a gently bred young lady. He sank down beside her on the bench, close enough that his thigh brushed presumptuously against her skirts. And then he looked at her. Really looked at her.

Damnation, but she was not an older lady at all. In fact, she appeared to be a relatively young woman. Her overlarge gown hung over what his practiced eye recognized as a slender and altogether pleasing frame. And the severe knot at the nape of her neck did nothing to disguise the light golden splendor of her hair. It was glossy and fair, several strands escaping their imprisonment to fall forward over her face and hands.

Small, elegant hands with delicately tapered fingers.

"Come now," Tristan said gruffly, "this won't do. You're weeping directly into your hands. Have you no handkerchief?" He extracted his own from the inner pocket of his greatcoat and offered it to her. "Here. Take mine."

She took it from him with trembling fingers, immediately clutching it to her face.

"Give me your spectacles," he commanded.

"M–my spectacles?" she asked.

He extended his hand. "I shall clean the lenses while you compose yourself."

She responded to his peremptory tone with the automatic obedience he expected from those in subordinate positions, removing her spectacles and dropping them into his outstretched hand. She then covered her face with his handkerchief once again.

Tristan examined the metal-framed spectacles with vague interest. They were bent and misshapen and, quite obviously, too large for her face. Secondhand, he decided, just like everything else she was wearing. He polished the wet lenses on the edge of his sleeve. When he had finished, he held them up to ascertain his handiwork, squinting as he looked through the lenses. They were as clean as he could get them. So clean that he could see right through them to the surrounding woods. He turned to look at her, his dark eyes narrowing with suspicion. "Either you and I suffer from the same abnormality of vision…or these lenses are made of clear glass."

"Oh, please go away, sir," she said on a sob.

He folded the spectacles and tossed them carelessly onto the seat beside him, well out of her reach. "I assume Lady Brightwell gave them to you."

That got her attention. She lowered the handkerchief, peering up at him over the edge of it with the loveliest pair of gray eyes Tristan had ever had the privilege to behold. "Do you… Do you know Lady Brightwell?" she ask in a husky, tear-clogged whisper.

And then her hands slowly dropped to her lap, taking the handkerchief with them.

Tristan stared at her, temporarily struck dumb. To say that her face was beautiful would not be entirely accurate. He had seen many beautiful women in his lifetime. Veritable goddesses.

The woman sitting in front of him now was no goddess.

She was, he realized somewhat nonsensically, more in line with being an angel.

Her face was ever so slightly heart-shaped. Her mouth full, soft, and unexpectedly kissable. Gently sculpted cheekbones, a straight, elegant nose, and gracefully winged brows several shades darker than her hair finished the picture.

And then there were those eyes. Wide, fathomless eyes. As stormy and tempest-tossed as the rain across an uncertain sea.

He swallowed hard. "Yes, I know Lady Brightwell," he said, far more harshly than he had intended. "And I recognize your breed as well. A companion, are you?"

"Yes."

"And these?" Tristan motioned to the spectacles. "Did they come with this revolting gown and this wretched…I dare not call it a coiffure." He frowned at her hair. "It's a sort of uniform, I take it. Lady Brightwell's uniform for a lady's companion."

"Yes," she admitted. She brought his handkerchief to her face and, quite energetically, blew her nose.

Tristan had never seen a lady attend to the business in such a matter-of-fact manner. "No woman would wear them by choice," he said. "Especially not a young lady like yourself."

"I'm not a young lady."

He raised his brows. "No? How old are you then, madam? Thirty? Forty?"

"Six and twenty."

He knew he was being rude to her, but couldn't seem to stop himself. "Six and twenty? So, not a young woman after all."

She completed drying her tears and then, for the first time, turned to look at him directly. What must, under better circumstances, be a rather enviable porcelain complexion was splotchy with weeping and her perfectly proportioned little nose shone red as a beacon. "How old are you, sir?" she enquired sharply. "Fifty? Sixty?"

Tristan was surprised into a crack of laughter.

She did not smile. She merely looked at him, her expression as reproving as a schoolteacher's.

He felt a twinge of remorse. It was a novel sensation. A deuced uncomfortable one, too. "I'm two and thirty," he informed her. "Practically in my dotage." He paused before adding, a tad roughly, "I beg your pardon if I have offended you. My only excuse is that, in the past, when confronted with a female in tears, I have often found incivility to be a great restorative. I suppose with you I must needs try some other remedy."

"Pray don't."

"You'd prefer I go?"

"Yes." She looked like she would have said more, but a slight breeze stirred the crumpled paper at her feet. Recalling its presence on the ground, she paled. She moved to pick it up, but Tristan anticipated her, reaching out and sweeping the crumpled paper up in his hand. "Oh don't!" she cried.

"What is this, then?" he asked as he flattened out the paper. "A love letter?"

She held out her hand for it, but he moved it just out of reach. "Give it back!" she demanded. "It's private! You have no right!"

"I daresay," he muttered. But having smoothed out the paper, he realized that it was not a love letter at all. It was an ink smudged drawing and a few lines of text which read:

> *My beloved speaks and says to me:*
> *Arise, my love, my fair one,*
> *and come away;*
> *for now the winter is past,*
> *the rain is over and gone.*

There was more, but it was illegible. It looked as if the inkwell had spilled over it, obscuring not only the remaining words, but part of the drawing as well.

"Please give it back to me," she begged him.

"What is this?" he asked, genuinely curious. "A poem you're writing?"

Her slender frame stiffened with something that may well have been outrage. "A poem! How can you say so? Don't you recognize it, sir?"

Tristan shrugged one broad shoulder. "I can't say that I do."

"It's the Song of Solomon. From the *Bible*."

"Ah, that explains my unfamiliarity." He frowned, reading the words once again. "The winter is past. The rain is over." He looked up at her. "What did the rest say? This part here where you have spilled ink?"

"I did not spill any ink!"

"No?"

She dashed away a fresh tear with the back of her hand. "The part that's ruined—the part just there—it was an earlier verse."

"Ah. I see."

She cast him another reproachful glance. Clearly she thought he should know it already. As if he might recite a Bible verse as easily as the latest music hall ballad. As easily as she recited it to him now:

> *"Set me as a seal upon thine heart,*
> *as a seal upon thine arm:*
> *for love is strong as death—"*

An unaccountable rush of warmth crept up his neck. He cut her off before she could say another word. "That's from the *Bible*?"

"Yes."

Tristan cleared his throat. "Well. It is rather…"

"It's beautiful," she declared.

Beautiful. Perhaps it was. What did he know of the Bible? He had read it, of course. He was a well-educated gentleman, after all. A well-bred one, too. As a boy, he'd even attended Sunday services with his father and brother at the family seat in Hampshire. He well recalled the hours spent sitting in the family pew, affecting a dutiful interest in the dry, toneless hymns and the long drawn-out sermons.

But that was a lifetime ago. In the years since, no one had had the temerity to spout verses or psalms at him. Not that any of his confederates would do so. Most of them were as sunken into depravity as he was himself. "Who is it for?" he asked. "Some beau of yours?"

She lunged for it and, before he could lift it out of her reach, snatched the paper from his hand and pressed it safely to her bosom. "How dared you." Her low voice was heated with indignation. "It's going to be a book of verses. An illustrated book of verses. It's not for *some beau.*"

And then she began to weep all over again.

Tristan felt a queer tightening in his chest. "My dear girl, what the devil are you carrying on about? Did one of Lady Fairford's footmen force a kiss on you? Or was it Lord Fairford himself?" The very thought made him inexplicably angry. "Confound it. Did no one warn you to be careful here?"

She wiped at her remaining tears with his sodden handkerchief. "Yes. Lady Brightwell said I must take care never to be alone with any of the gentlemen at the house party. But it...it wasn't a gentleman who upset me so."

Tristan winced. "One of the ladies, was it?"

"Yes. Lady Brightwell's daughter. Felicity."

"Bloody hell."

She gasped at his language. "Sir!"

Tristan was unrepentant. "Are you saying that Miss Bright-well...?" He ran a hand through his already disheveled black hair. The very idea! He'd known that Felicity Brightwell was forward and a bit wild, but he would never have guessed that her tastes ran to women. Come to that, he would never have guessed that Miss Brightwell would even be here. She was a chit of one and twenty and still actively seeking a husband. Or so he'd been led to believe. "Good God, what did she do to you?"

She shook her head. "I've already said too much."

"You've hardly said anything." He paused, watching her. "And why not? Do you fear I'll betray your confidence? I assure you, Lady Brightwell and her daughter are no friends of mine. And even if they were, your secrets would be safe with me."

"I shouldn't even be sitting with you like this."

"You're not sitting with me. I'm sitting with you."

She looked up at him with an expression that was both grave and damnably prim. It struck him quite suddenly that she bore more than a passing resemblance to a pretty little nun.

He wondered if she kissed like a nun as well.

"It doesn't matter who is sitting with whom," she said. "We haven't been properly introduced. I don't even know who you are."

This was a rare turn of events. If Lady Brightwell had taken to warning her new companion about rakes, rogues,

16

and vile seducers of women, surely his own name would have been at the top of the list. And even if it hadn't been, what woman in England didn't know of the infamous Viscount St. Ashton?

But then, he didn't look much like a viscount now, did he?

"Tristan Sinclair," he said brusquely. He waited for a reaction, but her face betrayed no hint of recognition. Doubtless it would if he added his title. Which was precisely why he did not. "And your name, ma'am?"

"Valentine March."

Tristan felt another uncomfortable quake in his heart. By God but it suited her. "I've never before met a woman named Valentine."

Miss March's cheeks flushed a delicate shade of pink. "Yes…well…my mother expected I would be a boy, you see. She only chose the one name. After St. Valentine. And then, when Mama died, Papa couldn't bring himself to call me anything else."

"Your mother died in childbed?"

Her blush deepened. "Yes."

Tristan nodded. "My own mother, as well. She succumbed not long after bringing my younger brother into the world." Good Lord! He never mentioned his mother. Not to his family. Not to his friends. Not to anyone. Her death was certainly no secret, but the very idea that he'd speak of her to a stranger— What in blazes was the matter with him?

"Well, Miss March," he said. "Now we're acquainted, you may tell me all your troubles."

Miss March looked down at the ink-stained paper, a line of distress appearing across the smooth surface of her brow.

"How long have you been in Lady Brightwell's employ?" he asked. "It can't have been more than a year, for last season she had a different companion. Wearing the same gown and spectacles, I'll wager."

"For two months."

"Why?"

She blinked up at him. "I beg your pardon?"

"Couldn't you have found a position with someone respectable?"

"But I understood that Lady Brightwell *was* respectable. I was recommended to her by Mrs. Pilcher, the squire's wife in our village. She and Lady Brightwell are friends, and Mrs. Pilcher had promised my father that…that when he was gone…that she would see I was taken care of."

"Your father is dead as well."

It hadn't been a question, but she answered it. There was a decided tremor in her voice. "Yes. Last year. He took a chill while out visiting his parishioners and, though I tried, I could not make him well again."

Tristan's brows snapped together. Hell's teeth, she was a vicar's daughter. No wonder she looked like a beatific little nun. "And this is your first position. Your first time hiring yourself out as a companion."

She nodded.

"Why hire yourself out at all? Why not marry? Surely there must have been any number of men in your village anxious to win your hand."

Her gaze lowered to the crumpled handkerchief in her hand. "There was no one," she said very quietly.

Tristan had the feeling that she was not being entirely truthful, but he didn't press her. "And no family?"

She hesitated a fraction of a second before saying again, "No one."

"And so you hired yourself out as a companion to Lady Hortensia Brightwell. A pity you and I weren't acquainted then. I might have warned you. Lady Brightwell attends only the raciest house parties, you know. The kind with drunken orgies and lecherous gentleman creeping into random bed-chambers in the middle of the night."

Miss March's face drained of color.

"And if you think your atrocious costume will protect your virtue, you're much mistaken. Many of the gentlemen in attendance would consider your spectacles and outsized gown a challenge." Tristan paused, wondering briefly if he was one such gentleman. "I hope you've been keeping your bedroom door locked, Miss March."

"We only arrived this morning. But I shall lock my door tonight, sir. I-I thank you for your warning."

He felt like an utter ass. "See that you do. And stay clear of Lady Brightwell's daughter. If she attempts to meddle with you again—"

"Meddle with me?" Her winged brows flew up in alarm.

"Touch you."

"Oh, she didn't touch *me*, Mr. Sinclair. I would have pre-ferred it if she had. A bruise might heal, but what she's done to my drawings…" Her gray eyes shimmered with unshed tears. "It can never be mended. She's ruined them."

"Your drawings," he repeated. And then he understood. Curse him for his depraved mind! Felicity Brightwell hadn't been forcing indecent attentions on her mother's companion. She'd been bullying and tormenting her. Making her life a misery. Naturally she would, for even in a drab gown and outsized spectacles, Valentine March outshone her.

"May I?" He reached out for the paper that she clutched so resolutely to her bosom. She relaxed her hold on it, making no objection as he plucked it from her fingers. He looked at it for a moment, his eyes skimming again the barely legible script.

Arise, my love, my fair one,
And come away;
For now the winter is past,
The rain is over and gone.

For some reason he couldn't explain, Tristan felt the beginnings of a lump in his throat. "It's not entirely ruined," he said gruffly. "You can still—"

"Oh, you don't understand!" Miss March cried. "This is the only one I could salvage! The rest are covered in ink. She poured it all over them. And then she laughed." She pressed her hands to her face.

"She is a rather unpleasant young lady." Tristan grimaced. Was that all he could come up with? Where were his honeyed tones? His caressing words? That famous St. Ashton address? "I take it that those drawings were very precious to you."

"More precious than anything in the whole world. They're all I had left of my—" She broke off. "Oh, it doesn't matter anymore! Nothing matters anymore."

"You can't start over? Draw them again?"

Miss March glanced up at him. Her eyes were bleak with despair. "No. Some of the drawings… They weren't mine, don't you see? I was only copying the verses. And now…" She didn't finish. Instead she retrieved her paper from him and once again clutched it to her chest. "I can't start over. Not alone. Besides, what would be the point? She would only ruin them again. Indeed, she said that the next time she caught me scribbling, she'd throw my work into the fire."

Tristan didn't know what to say to that. What could he say? She was an impoverished lady's companion. She was also a vicar's daughter. Even if he could summon up his trademark charm, what use would it be on someone like her? "Perhaps," he said at last, "Miss Brightwell will marry soon."

Miss March shivered. "Undoubtedly so, but what—"

"You're trembling," Tristan interrupted. His expression grew dark. "And no wonder. Out of doors in November without a bonnet, gloves or cloak. Have you no respect for the Yorkshire weather?" He began to remove his greatcoat. "Just because this estate is sheltered from the worst of it doesn't mean you still won't catch your death of cold. In case you hadn't noticed, it's been raining for three days straight."

Miss March watched him, wide-eyed, as he divested himself of his greatcoat. "I ran out of the house in rather a hurry.

There was no time to find gloves or a bonnet or— Oh!" She drew back from him. "What are you doing?"

Tristan paused, his greatcoat held open in his hands, poised to drape around her. "Lending you my coat, you little fool."

Her bosom rose and fell on an unsteady breath, but she made no further objection as he settled it around her shoulders. "Thank you," she said. "It's quite warm."

Tristan moved away from her. "I should think so. I've been wearing it the better part of the morning."

His words brought a fierce blush to her cheeks.

At another time, in another place, he might have laughed. A woman so innocent that the very thought of a man's body heat put her to the blush? A fine joke, to be sure. But as he looked at Valentine March, swallowed up in the folds of his caped greatcoat, he did not feel very much like laughing. Instead, he felt an aching swell of tenderness. It was so disconcerting that he almost swore aloud.

"What difference does it make if Miss Brightwell is married?" she asked.

Tristan rubbed the side of his face in an effort to collect his scattered thoughts. The scratch of uneven stubble abraded his palm. He had sent his valet, Higgins, ahead with the carriage. As a result, this morning at the inn he had been obliged to shave himself. And done a damned poor job of it, too. "When she marries, she'll go to her husband's house. Then you'll see her but rarely, I imagine."

"She *is* looking for a husband," Miss March conceded. "It's why we've come to this house party."

Tristan's mouth curved in a sardonic smile. "If that's so, Lady Brightwell isn't half the matchmaker I thought her to be."

"Why do you say so?"

"There are no gentlemen at Lord and Lady Fairford's house parties who are suitable for marriage. They invite only those of their same ilk. Inveterate gamblers, rakes, reprobates. The dissolute dregs of polite society."

"That can't be true, for Lady Brightwell said specifically that she brought Miss Brightwell here to further her interests with a particular gentleman. I believe he's considered to be a great matrimonial prize."

Tristan's eyes were already upon her, but at her words his gaze sharpened. "And who might this unfortunate soul be? Did Lady Brightwell name him?"

"Viscount St. Ashton." She looked up at him. "He's not one of those bad sorts of gentlemen you mentioned, is he? The rakes and the reprobates?"

Tristan gave a humorless laugh. It was a hoarse and bitter sound, edged with something very like anger. "My dear, Miss March," he said. "The Viscount St. Ashton is the biggest rake and reprobate of them all."

Chapter Two

Heat rushed to Valentine's face. It was all she could do not to press her hands against her scalding cheeks to cool her blushes. "Oh dear," she whispered. "You know him."

Mr. Sinclair was no longer laughing. "Intimately," he said.

She wished she might fall through the floor. And considering the dilapidated state of the folly, such an event was not entirely impossible. "Do forgive me, sir. Had I known he was your friend, I would never have said anything. Indeed, I shouldn't even be—"

"Sitting with me. Talking with me. Yes, I do believe we've established that, Miss March." His expression had been hard and stern, cold enough to scare her for an instant, but now it softened. "Never mind. You've said nothing to offend me."

Valentine looked at her companion. It was ridiculous to feel so at ease with a stranger. And yet he'd put her at ease from the moment he entered the folly and sat down beside her. Funny that. He hadn't been particularly nice to her. Indeed, he'd been brusque and commanding, ordering her about until she got her tears under control. He'd insulted her, too. At least, he'd insulted her gown and her rather unflattering coiffure.

And he'd thought The Song of Solomon was a love poem!

Clearly his education was somewhat lacking. Which was quite odd since he seemed to be very much a gentleman. A brutish sort of gentleman, to be sure, but a gentleman nonetheless. He must live on a neighboring estate. Perhaps he was some manner of country gentry? His clothes were cut well enough, for all that they were stained with mud, grass, and sweat. And he carried himself with an air of importance, even if his thick black hair was disheveled and there was a shadow of stubble on his strong, chiseled jaw and over the enticingly sensual curve of his lip.

Indeed, he was outrageously handsome. Perhaps the most handsome man Valentine had ever seen. Not that she'd seen very many. But surely few could compete with Mr. Sinclair's great height, broad shoulders, and smoldering dark eyes.

And she would have had to be blind not to notice that his breeches clung to long, powerfully made legs.

Or that his hands, when he snatched away her paper, had appeared to be twice the size of her own.

When he laughed, she'd even seen a flash of strong, white teeth. A bit wolfish, that laugh. A bit strange. But then, she didn't pretend to understand subtle society humor. Not that Mr. Sinclair was anything like the foppish drawing room exquisites she'd encountered during her first month working for Lady Brightwell.

And he was certainly nothing at all like Phil. But then, Phillip Edgecombe was slight of build, with the vaguely sickly pallor of a romantic poet. It had been the very quality that set all the girls in the village swooning over him.

"*You do understand, don't you Val?*" he'd said the last time they saw each other. "*Some things are simply not meant to be.*"

They'd been standing outside of the vicarage as two burly men unloaded a cart containing the furniture and various odds and ends belonging to the new vicar and his family. Valentine's own small trunk sat at her feet. "*Yes, Phil,*" she'd said numbly. "*I understand.*"

"*It doesn't mean I love you any less. And it doesn't mean we can't still be friends. Indeed, I shall write you as often as I can.*" He'd caught hold of her hand then, clutching it fervently in his. "*And if anything changes— If you should hear anything at all— You must write me immediately. Promise me, Val.*"

No. Tristan Sinclair was nothing like Phillip Edgecombe. He didn't disguise his true intentions with silky words and flattery. He was a brutally honest gentleman. A thoroughly masculine one, too. The kind Valentine suspected could only be found in the rural countryside. A gentleman farmer, she decided. God particularly approved of farmers. At least, Papa had always said so.

"Surely Lord St. Ashton can't be as bad as you say," she replied at last. "Else why would Lady Brightwell bring Miss Brightwell to meet him?"

"The Viscount St. Ashton is the Earl of Lynden's son and heir. That fact alone makes him irresistible—and has done since he was a lad of eighteen."

Valentine considered this with a furrowed brow. "Yes. I did hear Lady Brightwell likening him to some rare beast that has evaded capture for far too many years. I didn't regard it. It's simply how Lady Brightwell talks. She is…rather candid."

"She's vulgar."

"Oh." Valentine frowned. She'd thought all aristocratic ladies spoke in the manner of Lady Brightwell and her daughter. "Do you really think so?"

"Everyone in attendance at this house party of yours is vulgar." He gave her a wry smile. "Everyone save yourself and one other."

"Who is the other?"

"The Earl of Lynden."

She blinked in surprise. "Lord St. Ashton's father? I had no idea he'd be in attendance. Lady Brightwell hasn't mentioned—"

"He wasn't invited. Even if he had been, he would never attend this sort of party."

"Then why…?"

"He's come here for the sole purpose of surprising his wayward heir. I expect a confrontation later this afternoon. No doubt some ultimatum will be involved."

"An ultimatum? I don't understand."

"The earl's younger son married last year. His wife recently presented him with a son. Meanwhile, St. Ashton is still unmarried. He's made no attempts to secure the line. I daresay

Lynden fears his heir will never wed. Or that, if he does, it'll be to some music hall performer. Or worse."

"If that's the alternative, then it's lucky for Lord St. Ashton that Miss Brightwell is in attendance. He can simply make her an offer of marriage and—"

"Is that what you advise?" he asked sharply.

Valentine blushed. "I-I have no advice."

"You must have. You're acquainted with Miss Brightwell. Tell me, would she make a good wife? A good viscountess?"

Valentine had already said too much about Miss Brightwell. It was bad enough that she privately loathed her. To be airing her grievances to strangers was well-nigh unforgiveable. Not to mention profoundly unchristian. She was supposed to love her neighbor. Turn the other cheek and so forth. It was how she'd been raised. Oh, how disappointed Papa would be if he could see her now. Sitting with a strange man unchaperoned. Gossiping about the very employer whose wages kept her from the workhouse.

Well, perhaps not the *workhouse*. She wasn't that badly off. Not yet, anyway.

"I'm sure she would make a creditable viscountess," Valentine managed to say.

Mr. Sinclair didn't look very convinced. "Creditable," he repeated. "The very girl who destroyed what you hold most precious in the world."

Valentine stared down at what was left of her book of Bible verses. She'd almost managed to come to terms with the disastrous events that had driven her to the folly, but, at Mr. Sinclair's words, she felt the full, oppressive weight of her servitude descend once more over her shoulders. Tears stung at the backs of her eyes. "What does it matter how she's treated me? I'm only a companion. Not much better than a servant, really."

"Miss March," Mr. Sinclair said quietly, "I—"

"There you are!" a man's voice called out. "Higgins said I might find you here."

Valentine looked up with a start to see a florid-faced gentleman approach. She recognized him as Lord Quinton. An impeccably dressed, middle-aged libertine who bore on his reddened visage the marks of a life spent indulging in all manner of vices. He was a particular friend of Lady Brightwell, who'd grudgingly introduced him to Valentine earlier that morning in the front hall of Fairford House.

"And who's that with you?" Lord Quinton briefly squinted in her direction, clearly not recognizing her without her spectacles. He grinned at Mr. Sinclair. "I say, St. Ashton. After all these years, you still don't miss a trick. Not an hour in the place and already out in the woods with a willing female."

Valentine shot up from her seat and straight out of Mr. Sinclair's greatcoat. It fell from her shoulders, dropping to the debris-covered floor to pool around her feet. Mr. Sinclair rose just as rapidly. He reached out to her, but she instinctively backed away, her shoulders bumping into one of the splintered pillars of the folly. Her heart beat a rapid, panicked rhythm in her chest. It fairly stole her breath away. "Y-you are Lord St. Ashton?"

"If you'll allow me to explain—"

"Oh no," she said. "Oh, how *could* you."

Mr. Sinclair looked stricken. But it was not Mr. Sinclair at all. It was the Viscount St. Ashton. She could see the truth plainly on his face. He held her gaze as he took a step toward her. "Miss March—"

She flattened herself against the pillar.

"What in blazes is going on, St. Ashton?" Quinton asked in a great booming voice. He climbed the steps to join them. "Don't you know the earl's here? Back at the house waiting for you? Come, man, the sooner you speak with him the sooner he'll quit the place." Quinton's eyes came to rest on Valentine's face. "And then the real fun can begin."

Valentine lunged away from the pillar and ran down the steps, nearly falling over a broken board as she went. She thought she heard someone call out to her, "Miss March!" But she didn't heed it. She clutched her heavy skirts and ran through the woods as fast as her legs could carry her. Tree branches with wet leaves whipped at her face and body. Droplets of rainwater and mud spattered her gown and her hair. But she didn't stop. She kept running until she was within sight of the kitchen entrance to Fairford House.

Once there, she leaned against the wall outside the door, breathing heavily and clutching the stitch in her side with one trembling hand.

"You there!" someone shouted. "Ain't you Lady Bright-well's new companion?"

Valentine squeezed her eyes shut for a moment before answering. "Yes!"

"She's been asking for you this last hour. Ringing that bell of hers 'til she damned near broke the bell-pull."

Valentine looked at the young footman who addressed her. He was painfully thin with a self-important gleam in his small rat-like eyes.

"If I was you," he advised, "I'd have a care about losing me place."

"Yes, thank you. I shall go to Lady Brightwell at once." She moved toward the kitchen door, but he stepped in front of her.

"Not so fast," he said, eyeing her suspiciously. "You look different."

Valentine was at the limits of her endurance. "I'm not at all interested in your opinion of my appearance, sir."

The footman grinned, showing two chipped front teeth. "I know what it is. You've taken off them spectacles of yours."

"My spectacles?" Valentine's hand flew instinctively to her face. They were gone! She must have left them in the folly.

And suddenly, with a sickening sense of despair, she realized that her spectacles were not the only thing she'd left behind on her mad flight from the folly. The last remaining page of her book of Bible verses was there, too. She had dropped it when she leapt from her seat and forgotten it completely in her desperate dash back to the house.

Now it was as good as gone.

The last remnant of her mother's legacy to her.

Out there somewhere in the woods. At the mercy of one of the worst rakes in England.

Chapter Three

The library at Fairford House had seen better days. The carpets were worn, the chairs in desperate need of reupholstering, and the motley collection of books appeared not to have been dusted in an age. A newly made fire burned weakly in the grate, doing little to take the chill out of the room and even less to diminish the scent of damp, rotting wood.

"Fairford never was the bookish sort." Richard Augustus Sinclair, 6th Earl of Lynden, lowered himself into a poorly sprung armchair. It sagged under his weight. "Nor was his father."

Tristan leaned against the mantel, a porcelain figure of a frolicking fawn in his hand. He turned it in his fingers, idly examining the tasteless ornament before returning it to its brethren on the cluttered mantelshelf. "I had forgotten that you were acquainted with the last Baron Fairford."

"I knew of him. Can't say I was ever fool enough to accept an invitation to his home."

"Unlike me?"

Now in his late sixties, the Earl of Lynden looked every bit of his age. His hair had gone completely gray. His stern face was lined, his tall, broad-shouldered frame slightly bent under the weight of his years. This was a man who'd buried a much-beloved wife. A man who'd seen his youngest son return from fighting in the Crimea, damaged almost beyond repair. A hard man. And, at least in Tristan's experience, a damnably unforgiving one.

"Unlike you," Lord Lynden concurred.

Tristan folded his arms. The action played havoc with the line of his frock coat. Higgins would be none too pleased. He had just spent over an hour fussing about like a pestilent gnat while Tristan bathed, shaved, and dressed in a fresh suit of clothes. "I don't make it a habit," he said. "In truth, I've only accepted invitations here on two prior occasions. The last was more than two years ago."

"As I'm well aware. What I wonder is why you accepted this one."

"And what I wonder is how you found me. On the very day of my arrival, too. If I didn't know better, I would think I had a spy in my household."

Lord Lynden didn't deny it. "There are some amongst your staff who still have their heads on straight."

Tristan could not repress a scowl. No doubt it was that secretary of his. Musgrove. Confound his impudence. He was always popping his head up from his duties, spouting the most infernal advice. "He'll be looking for a new position soon," he muttered.

His father was unmoved. "Elizabeth expects the family down at Sinclair House for Christmas," he said. "I understand she wrote you a letter."

Tristan liked his brother's wife well enough, though what she saw in John, he had no idea. The two had married last year, igniting something of a scandal. A true love match, people said. Tristan didn't doubt it. He'd seen them together.

An experience he didn't care to repeat more often than he must.

There was something profoundly disquieting about his younger brother being settled happily in the country with his sweet, beautiful wife and infant son. It wasn't that Tristan begrudged them their happiness—God knew John deserved it after what he'd suffered during the war—but the sight of that happiness made Tristan's own life seem so incredibly empty by comparison.

"Is that the reason behind your sudden flight to North Yorkshire? A wish to avoid spending Christmas in Devonshire?"

"That would be an extreme reaction."

"For some. For you, it would be typical." Lord Lynden paused before asking, "Are you jealous of him?"

"Of John?" Tristan laughed. "Not likely."

"You could have the same as he has if you wanted it."

"A wife like Elizabeth? That's doubtful. Besides, you assume I want the life John has." Tristan turned his head to look at his father. "I ask you, when have I ever wished to retire permanently to the country?"

Lord Lynden contemplated his eldest son with a frown. "You may no longer have a choice."

"At last," Tristan murmured. "We get to the substance of your visit." He pushed himself from the mantel and moved leisurely to take a seat across from his father. "So what's it to be this time? Do you intend to exile me to the country?"

"It's not in my power to exile you."

"I believe it is, sir. The only property I own outright is Blackburn Priory."

"An estate you've neglected since I gave it to you on your twenty-first birthday."

Tristan felt his temper rising. The estate in Northumberland was an ongoing bone of contention between him and his father. "A falling-down heap in the middle of nowhere, which you expected a lad to remove to and revive single-handed."

"Not just any lad," Lord Lynden growled. "My son. My heir. Instead you've spent over a decade drinking and whoring and gambling away a fortune in cards. At five and twenty, I thought it was out of your system. And then at thirty and every year since. No more, I tell you. No more money. No more credit. If you wish an income, earn it from your own estate. Go to Northumberland and do what you should have done eleven years ago. I'll not see the earldom bankrupted by your vices."

Tristan had been expecting just such a threat. Nevertheless, his father's words chilled him to the bone. "You won't have failed to notice that my expenses have fallen dramatically in the past two years," he replied in a surprisingly steady voice. "I'm hardly bankrupting the earldom."

"No, indeed. It seems to me that you spend the majority of your time alone. Alone and drunk. That's what worries me most of all."

Damn Musgrove! Tristan fumed silently, imagining how satisfying it would be to throttle the man. Who else could have relayed such mortifying information to the earl? "My secretary has painted a grim picture for you. Though not, I regret, an entirely accurate one."

Lord Lynden's frown deepened. "Look at yourself, my boy. When have you last eaten properly? When have you slept? And then, to rouse yourself enough to come here, when you should be with your family. What the devil's the matter with you? I know that for once it's not a woman. That's something, at least. But by God, it's not enough, sir."

"I daresay if I took a wife and sired a passel of brats you'd feel differently."

"Perhaps once, but I've long given up my hopes of your choosing anyone suitable." Lord Lynden shook his head in defeat. "No. I've finished with you, Tristan. Go to Northumberland and do what you will there. Drink yourself into an early grave. Scatter the countryside with your by-blows—"

"My by-blows?" Tristan had the sudden urge to laugh. Or to cry. He didn't know which. "If this is more of the rot Musgrove's been feeding you, then let me tell you that he's got it wrong, sir."

"Has he."

"I've never sired even one bastard, let alone enough bastards to populate the county of Northumberland."

This revelation seemed to give Lord Lynden pause. "Not a one?" he asked with ill-disguised concern.

To Tristan's chagrin he felt himself turning a dull red. "I'm more than capable, sir," he bit out. "If you must know, I've always taken…precautions."

"Ah." Lord Lynden settled back in his chair with relief. "Frankly, that's more than I would have expected of you. But no matter. You may have failed in your duty to marry and set up your nursery, but John has not. As it stands, Charles will inherit the earldom when you and your brother are gone. And I intend to preserve it for him."

Charles Augustus Sinclair. Damnation, he was not even one year old! "I wouldn't be too hasty on that score," Tristan said. "Lest you forget, Charles is an infant and I'm a man in my prime. I may yet marry and sire a legitimate heir."

Lynden snorted. "I shall believe that when I see it."

"Even if I don't, I intend to live a good long while."

"At the rate you're going? Between the curricle races, the dueling, and the drink, you'll be lucky to live another ten years."

Tristan glared at him. It had been years since he participated in a carriage race. As for dueling… Bloody hell. That had been a single instance of stupidity at Oxford. A drunken lark at the age of seventeen. Shots had been fired, true, but to categorize it as a duel was a stretch. And he'd certainly never repeated the behavior. Not with pistols, at any rate.

"I see you've accounted for everything," he said at last.

"I have given the matter a great deal of thought."

"And how long do I have before you cut off my funds?"

"The first of the year seems reasonable enough, assuming you see your way to spending Christmas in Devonshire."

"And if I don't?"

"I shall send a wire to my secretary, instructing him that no more money is to be advanced to you and no more of your creditors are to be paid. Effective immediately."

Tristan reminded himself again that he'd expected this. That he'd known his father was nearing the end of his patience and that drastic action was soon to be forthcoming. The knowledge did nothing to prevent him from feeling as if his entire world had just been brutally upended. "So I'm to leave Devonshire after Christmas and make straight for Northumberland? With no funds at my disposal to repair the estate?"

"That's right."

"And what if I should marry before then?"

Lord Lynden folded his hands across his midsection. "In the next two weeks?" he asked with a chuckle of disbelief. "Do you have someone in mind?"

The short answer was no, but these were desperate times. Tristan promptly blurted out the first name that popped into his head: "Felicity Brightwell."

His father had plainly not been expecting an answer. And he had certainly not been expecting the one that Tristan gave him. "Hortensia Brightwell's chit?" His face darkened like a thundercloud. "By God, sir. Is that the sort of creature you imagine as the next Countess of Lynden? The lady to wear your mother's jewels? Preside over your mother's house?"

Again, the answer was no. Tristan could not see Felicity Brightwell wearing his mother's jewels—though she would undoubtedly relish doing so. Neither could he see her presiding over the great house in Hampshire. The truth was, he didn't like Felicity Brightwell at all. Though technically well bred, she was as vulgar as her mother. Not that he hadn't consorted with vulgar women before, but a wife was something different. A wife was meant to be gentle, gracious, intelligent, and kind.

Like his own mother had been.

Like John's wife was now.

Even so, he might have been able to stomach marrying Felicity Brightwell. He might even have been able to rouse himself to get an heir off of her.

Up until the moment he learned how she'd behaved toward Valentine March.

Tristan raked a hand through his hair, remembering the look on Miss March's face when that oaf Quinton had called him St. Ashton.

"Don't say you're in love with her," Lord Lynden scoffed.

"*What?*"

"The Brightwell chit."

"Oh. Her." Tristan rubbed his jaw. "No. I'm not in love with anyone. But Miss Brightwell is here."

"Here? In North Yorkshire?"

"Here in this house." Tristan ignored his father's exclamation of disapproval. "She's come here in pursuit of me, apparently."

"What the devil kind of unmarried female attends a gathering like this?"

"One who very much wants to be the next Countess of Lynden."

The Earl of Lynden looked at his son with blank outrage. "I'll not have it. Do you hear me? I'll not have it."

"You can hardly prevent it."

"Don't underestimate me, my boy." Lord Lynden rose from his chair, signaling the end of their interview.

Tristan stood as well and, in grim silence, followed his father to the library doors. It occurred to him that he should say something more in his defense. That he should argue with his father or even make an impassioned plea for some little leniency. But reasoning with his implacable sire had never yielded any results in the past. And abject pleading had only ever earned him a greater measure of his contempt. "When do you return to Hampshire?" he asked.

"At first light."

"And tonight? Has Lady Fairford arranged a room for you here?"

Lord Lynden's lip curled with disdain. As if the very thought of spending a night in such a den of iniquity was repellent to him. "I have taken rooms at the Golden Hind."

"Lord and Lady Fairford will expect you to stay for dinner at least."

"Dine? Here? Don't be absurd. I've a private parlor at the inn. I shall have my dinner there."

They emerged from the library into the main hall of Fairford House. Tristan opened his mouth to respond to his father, but at the unexpected sight of Valentine March he swallowed his words.

She was hurrying down the main staircase, the skirts of her gown clutched lightly in one hand and a folded Indian shawl in the other. She was without her spectacles, of course. She'd left them behind when she ran from the folly. But any improvement to her features was overshadowed by a new addition to her unflattering companion's uniform—a dowdy little cap that covered all but a few locks of her pale golden hair.

As she descended, she raised her head and their eyes met. She immediately looked away, continuing down the final few steps with an added burst of speed. As if she could not get away from him fast enough. As if she believed she might escape him as easily as she had when she ran from the folly.

He strode toward her, his father temporarily forgotten. "Miss March."

She came to an abrupt halt, the Indian shawl clutched tight to her bosom. "Lord St. Ashton." She sounded a trifle breathless. Whether from the exertion of running down the stairs or the anxiety of seeing him again, he could not tell. "I beg you would excuse me. I must take Lady Brightwell her shawl." She made a motion to walk past him.

Tristan moved instinctively to block her path. "A moment if you please."

"My lord?"

My lord. There was a wealth of meaning in that simple address. No doubt she thought he'd lied to her. That he'd been having a private laugh at her expense or, even worse, that he'd been embarking on a seduction. Though how she could imagine he was trying to seduce her, he had no idea. He'd approached her in the folly with a startling lack of finesse. Indeed, he could not recall having ever been so clumsy and churlish with a woman.

"I have your…" What the devil to call it? Her drawing? Her psalms? "Your paper," he said lamely. "The one you left behind in the folly."

She lifted her gaze to his with obvious unwillingness. Her gray eyes were shadowed with wariness and more than a little hurt.

Tristan felt again that same peculiar twinge of remorse he had felt in the folly. He brutally suppressed it. "It's safe in my room along with your spectacles," he said, sinking his voice. "If you like, I'll return them to you at dinner this evening."

"As you please, my lord."

"You *will* be present at dinner, I trust."

"Yes, my lord."

Tristan gritted his teeth. "You may cease 'my lording' me, Miss March. I did not lie to you. Not precisely. My name *is* Tristan Sinclair. I was about to tell you all when Quinton appeared. Had you given me one minute more—"

"You owe me no explanation."

"I think I do."

"Please let me pass, sir," she said softly.

"Miss March…"

"*Please* let me pass. We will be remarked."

He might have detained her longer, but what else could he say? Even if he had a mind to make his apologies, he could hardly do so in the middle of the hall. And as for seduction…

Good lord, was he seriously contemplating an affair with Miss March? She was a meek little lady's companion. A psalm-quoting vicar's daughter. And yet…

And yet, at that moment, still reeling from the terrific blow he'd been dealt by his father, Tristan would have given a great deal to take Valentine March in his arms.

He hesitated a second longer and then, reluctantly, stepped aside.

"Thank you," she said. And then, without a backward glance, she strode briskly past him down the corridor that led to the conservatory. Tristan stood, staring after her much as he had when she fled the folly.

When he turned back to his father, he found the earl watching him, an unreadable expression on his face.

"That was Miss March," Tristan explained gruffly. "She's Lady Brightwell's new companion."

"Another conquest?"

"Hardly. She's a vicar's daughter. When I met her, she even recited a psalm at me. Can you imagine?" Tristan managed a grim smile. "I daresay I've given her a disgust of me."

"A rarity."

He cast his father a weighted glance. "I introduced myself to her as Tristan Sinclair. When she discovered I was St. Ashton, she ran away."

Lord Lynden gave a grunt of approval. "Sounds like the gel has good sense."

"Good sense? She's a complete innocent. She shouldn't even be here. Anything could happen to her." Tristan's expression darkened. "You should have seen the way Quinton looked at her. The confounded villain. If he thinks that—"

"My lords!" Lady Fairford called to them as she entered the hall.

Tristan immediately schooled his features into a mask of slightly bored indifference and turned to greet his hostess. He couldn't help but notice that his father did the same.

Lady Fairford made her way toward them, a provocative swing in her step. She was a voluptuous brunette on the shady side of forty, known for indulging her insatiable appetites as freely as her lecherous husband did. "Just look at the two of you!" she exclaimed. "It's been years since I've seen you in a room together! How handsome you both look! And so very alike. What a coup it is that I shall have you both at my table this evening."

"I beg your pardon, ma'am," Tristan began, "but my father—"

"I look forward to it," Lord Lynden said. "And I'm pleased to tell you that my travel plans have changed. It appears I'll be staying in Yorkshire awhile longer. I trust you have room to accommodate me."

Tristan's eyes narrowed at his father. What the devil was he up to?

"You wish to stay *here*?" Lady Fairford's toothy smile turned a touch brittle. "How splendid! But perhaps you'd be more comfortable at the inn? Fairford House is not what it once was, you know. The rooms do get a bit drafty on occasion. I would hate for you to take ill."

"Rubbish," Lord Lynden declared. There was steel in his voice. "A room here will suit me very well, madam. If you'll only direct me to it, I shall retire until dinner."

Tristan almost felt sorry for Maria Fairford. The house party would hardly be able to continue as normal under the Earl of Lynden's disapproving eye. Unfortunately, given his present circumstances, Tristan was in no position to do anything about it. He was as much at his father's mercy as everyone else was.

Chapter Four

"How could you be so thoughtless?" asked Lady Brightwell again. "To run out into the woods and lose your spectacles in such a careless manner?"

"I wasn't thinking particularly clearly at the time," Valentine replied.

She stood at the edge of Lady Brightwell's bedroom, watching as a browbeaten lady's maid put the final touches on Lady Brightwell's hair. Felicity Brightwell lounged in a chair, her frothy pink evening gown glaringly at odds with the faded furnishings.

Valentine had been given a small room of her own on the third floor. A room that couldn't be much larger than a medieval nun's cell. It had a narrow little iron bed, a rickety washstand, and a wooden chest of drawers, which had given her a splinter in her finger the second she touched it. There was no mirror, of course. Not that she couldn't guess what it would have revealed.

She'd dressed for dinner in a gown of serviceable gray silk. And it truly was her own gown. The village seamstress had made it for her three years ago in Hartwood Green. She could still remember how Papa had grumbled at the expense. But though it fit her a great deal better than Lady Brightwell's shapeless sacks, it was still far from fashionable. The color was plain, the neckline overly modest, and it had a conspicuous lack of flounces and frills. Indeed, she feared she looked very much like what she was.

A vicar's daughter.

She told herself she did not care. And why should she? What difference did it make if the guests here thought she was a drab little dowd? They were no friends of hers. And she'd never taken undue pride in her looks. Although…

Although she'd spent an inordinate amount of time brushing her hair to a flaxen shine and smoothing the wrinkles from her silken skirts, all the while wondering what Lord St. Ashton would think when he saw her.

No doubt it was a weakness inherited from her mother. How else to explain it? She was not a wanton. And Papa had raised her better than to lower her guard at the first advance of a practiced rake. Not that St. Ashton had advanced. Indeed, the more she reflected on their encounter the more she recognized how abominably rude he had been to her.

Except that he had given her his handkerchief.

And he had draped his greatcoat over her shoulders with something very like reverence.

Oh, what a fool she was to even entertain such thoughts! The Viscount St. Ashton had no interest in her. Well…perhaps he was mildly interested, but only in the way a cat might be interested in batting at an injured mouse. And she was not so naïve as to mistake cruel amusement for anything like genuine interest in her as a person.

Not for the first time, she called up an image of how he'd appeared when he approached her in the hall. Any resemblance to country gentry had vanished. Instead, he'd looked urbane and aristocratic. Altogether intimidating.

"And why were you away so long?" Lady Brightwell demanded. "It must have been an hour before you returned to the house."

"Longer, Mama," Felicity said under her breath. "For you summoned her and she couldn't be found."

"Longer than an hour?" Lady Brightwell gave a pout of displeasure. "Whatever could you have been doing for such a time?" She met Valentine's eyes in the mirror of her looking glass. "I trust you were not dallying with one of the footmen."

Valentine colored. "Indeed not, ma'am."

It was not entirely a lie. The Viscount St. Ashton was no footman. And the two of them had certainly not been dallying.

"I suppose you were upset over that silly business with your little sketches." Lady Brightwell sighed. "I warned you that Felicity was high spirited, didn't I? I can't think why you provoked her. Especially when she's so overwrought about this business with St. Ashton."

"I'm not overwrought, Mama," Felicity objected. "Why should I be?"

"No reason, my darling. But do listen, I beg you. You must keep a tighter rein on your temper. These tantrums of yours are terribly unbecoming. I insist you apologize to Miss March so we can put the whole business behind us."

Felicity folded her arms and scowled. It seemed, for a moment, as if she wouldn't obey her mother. However, after a prolonged pout, she did as she was bid. "I beg your pardon, Miss March. But Mama is right. You shouldn't have provoked me. If you'd only come when I called to you, I wouldn't have lost my temper."

A poor apology. A non-apology, in fact. Valentine bowed her head in silent acknowledgment.

"There now," Lady Brightwell said, patting her curls into place. "We'll speak of it no more."

Valentine clasped her hands in front of her. She couldn't so easily forget what had happened. Indeed, the very thought of thirty pages' worth of her mother's sketches and Bible verses damaged beyond repair was enough to bring tears to her eyes once again. But she'd resolved not to cry anymore. It accomplished nothing. She would do better to look to her future.

"Miss March?" Lady Brightwell gestured with an imperious hand. "Fetch my jewel case. I think I will wear my ruby necklace this evening. Or perhaps my brooch."

Valentine obediently collected the small case of jewels and brought it for Lady Brightwell's perusal. Felicity leapt up to join her mother, and the two of them were soon well occupied with the serious business of jewelry selection. Valentine withdrew to the corner of the room again as Lady Brightwell and her daughter preened in front of the glass.

They were as alike in looks as any mother and daughter could be. Both with the same sable hair and dark flashing eyes. Both with well-shaped figures and milky skin. The only dissimilarity, besides their obvious difference in age, was that Lady Brightwell had a perpetually vacant expression whereas Felicity always appeared as if she'd just encountered a bad smell.

Would St. Ashton truly consider marrying her? Lady Brightwell certainly thought he would. And Felicity shared her mother's opinion. But when Valentine had talked with him earlier, he'd professed a dislike for Lady Brightwell and her daughter. Not that anything he'd said in the folly had been the truth.

"What about Miss March's spectacles, Mama?" Felicity demanded. "You can't let her go down to dinner barefaced."

"There's nothing that can be done about that now. We must all make the best of it." Lady Brightwell rose from her chair and shook the skirts of her gown over her wire crinoline. "That doesn't mean you're absolved, Miss March. Tomorrow morning, you must go out into the woods and locate your spectacles. Pray they're not lost or damaged, for I'll have to take the cost out of your wages."

Valentine opened her mouth to object and then promptly shut it again. There was no need to protest the unfairness of such a decree. St. Ashton had her spectacles, after all. He'd promised to return them to her at dinner. Though she didn't see how he could. The likelihood of the two of them having a moment alone was less than zero.

"Mama, did you speak to Lady Fairford about the seating arrangements?"

"You have nothing to worry about, pet," Lady Brightwell assured her. "You'll be on St. Ashton's right and Mrs. Ravenscroft will be on his left."

Mrs. Ravenscroft was a well-preserved widow of fifty and, according to the Fairfords' cook, Mrs. Gaunt, only attended the annual house parties to meet with Lord Horsham, her elderly married beau.

"That Mrs. Ravenscroft don't engage in any of them lewd games her ladyship puts on," Mrs. Gaunt had gossiped cheerfully as she sat with Valentine in the kitchen that afternoon sharing a pot of tea. "She's only here for Lord Horsham and him for her."

Mrs. Gaunt had told Valentine about the other guests as well, warning her which gentlemen she must stay away from at all costs and which of the ladies it would be best to avoid. Afterward, Valentine had felt guilty for sitting and gossiping with a servant. She was a gentlewoman and, as a lady's companion, not technically a servant herself. It would not do to fall into bad habits. But Mrs. Gaunt had been so kind.

And her disclosures about St. Ashton had been impossible to resist.

"As handsome a devil as ever there was," she'd said. "He's not one who has to force anyone to his bed. They come willingly enough, by twos and threes, or so I've heard."

"By twos and threes?" Valentine's eyes had widened. "Do you mean…two and three ladies in his bed all at once?"

Mrs. Gaunt had given a knowing nod. "It was before my time, mind you. I only come here two years ago. But I heard the stories from every giggling housemaid who ever crossed his path."

"Oh, but surely he doesn't…?"

"Meddle with the servants?" Mrs. Gaunt had cackled. "No fear of that, dearie. He's one of them lords as is too high in the instep for the likes of us."

The likes of us.

Valentine had heard the words with a decided pang in her heart, knowing she'd been automatically included in the group of servants and other unsuitable females St. Ashton considered beneath him. Not that it mattered a jot. She hadn't taken employment only to fall victim to some rake. She had a plan for her future. A respectable, virtuous plan that only required a small bit of money. The annual sum of her wages as a lady's companion, in fact. In ten more months she would have it.

And then…

"St. Ashton will have nothing to say to Mrs. Ravenscroft," Felicity said, her sullen voice recalling Valentine back to the present. "She's a dried-up old crone."

"She's my age, my love," Lady Brightwell said. "I hope you don't think me an old crone."

"No, but Mama, I thought I was to sit between St. Ashton *and* his father."

"Perhaps tomorrow. He'll be staying the week, I understand. Maria Fairford is up in arms. Her party games can't commence while he's present." Lady Brightwell sighed. "It's regrettable. Lord Penworthy's here, and he and I have always been on especially good terms."

"Mama!"

"Come, my love," Lady Brightwell said, oblivious to her daughter's scandalized gasp. "We must make an appearance in the drawing room before dinner. Miss March? Don't dawdle."

Valentine followed in their wake as they exited Lady Brightwell's bedroom and swept down the stairs to the second floor. They arrived in the drawing room amidst a crush of other guests who were dressed in their evening finery. There were over a dozen gentlemen, ranging from their middle twenties to as old as seventy, if Valentine was any judge, while most of the ladies in attendance seemed to be upwards of forty. They made a merry party, all appearing to know each other and falling swiftly into murmured reminiscences of prior house parties.

"St. Ashton!" Felicity called suddenly. "Look, Mama! There he is with the Earl of Lynden." She raised her hand and wiggled her gloved fingers. "St. Ashton!"

He towered head and shoulders over most of the gentlemen in the room. Valentine could easily make him out. For a moment, she considered ducking out of the drawing room and sprinting back upstairs. But it was too late. The Viscount St. Ashton was already making his way toward them.

He was clad in the most elegant evening attire she'd ever beheld. A fitted black evening coat and trousers, embroidered waistcoat, and snowy white linen that sparkled in the candlelight. His black hair was brushed into meticulous order, his side-whiskers trimmed short beneath the hard planes of his cheekbones. His face was composed into lines of fashionably bored indifference. Only his mouth betrayed any emotion. It was edged with what she could only describe as a sardonic smile.

It sent a shiver of unease through her.

"St. Ashton, how very bad of you to hide yourself away all afternoon," Felicity chastised the viscount when he came to stand before them. "Didn't you know I was here? You might have sent for me. We could have gone for a drive or taken a walk."

St. Ashton greeted mother and daughter with civility, if not friendliness. "The weather would hardly have supported either," he said.

"Nonsense. My mother's companion was out walking in the woods earlier this afternoon." Felicity glanced back at Valentine, who'd shielded herself from view behind the two much taller ladies. "Weren't you, Miss March?"

An expression of surprise flickered across St. Ashton's face and then was gone. "Ah, Miss March. I didn't see you hiding back there."

"My lord."

"And were you out walking in the woods?"

She had the distinct impression he was amusing himself at her expense again. "I was. It was an exceedingly unpleasant experience."

St. Ashton flashed a grin. "Hardly a recommendation. Wouldn't you say, Miss Brightwell?" He didn't wait for Felicity to answer. Instead, he offered his arm to her mother. "I beg your indulgence, ma'am. My father has a wish to renew his acquaintance with you and your daughter before we go in to dinner."

Lady Brightwell beamed. "Naturally he would. Felicity, my pet, come along."

Valentine hesitated, watching the three of them walk away. Once again, she considered bolting.

And once again St. Ashton thwarted her.

"You too, Miss March," he said, not even bothering to look back at her.

"Oh, but he wouldn't like to meet my mother's *companion*," Felicity said. She linked her hand through St. Ashton's free arm, clinging to him like a limpet. "Won't he be insulted, my lord? To be sure, *I* think he will."

"You don't know my father, Miss Brightwell," St. Ashton replied.

Lord Lynden was seated close to the fireplace. With his hard, humorless features and iron-gray hair, he appeared far more intimidating than his rakish son. He rose at their approach, his mouth set in a grim line as Lady Brightwell introduced him to her daughter and her companion.

"Miss March," Lord Lynden said.

"My lord," she replied.

He gave her a long, penetrating look. "You're from Surrey, I understand." It was not a question.

Valentine felt for a moment as if the shabby drawing room carpet had been pulled out from under her slippered feet. She met the Earl of Lynden's eyes. They were dark and unreadable. And yet, she hadn't even the smallest doubt.

He knew.

"Yes, my lord," she answered him. Her mouth had gone dry as cotton wool. She steeled herself for more questions, but the earl merely gave a thoughtful-sounding harrumph.

She prayed that he'd lost interest in her and, indeed, he seemed to do so. The remainder of his time in the drawing room was spent listening to Felicity and Lady Brightwell reminiscing about their last season in London. He didn't pay Valentine any attention at all.

But any hope she had that the Earl of Lynden had forgotten her was swiftly dispelled at the moment Lady Fairford announced dinner.

"No need to bother with precedence," she said with a shrill laugh. "We are quite informal here."

"Miss March." Lord Lynden offered her his arm. "I shall escort you into the dining room."

Valentine's palms grew damp beneath her gloves. She wished she were the sort of lady who swooned. If she were, she could have fainted dead away and been excused to her room for the evening. Instead, she put her hand lightly on Lord Lynden's arm and allowed him to lead her in to the dining room.

Once there, he waited as she settled in her place.

And then, to her alarm, he took the seat beside her.

***

No gentleman who had just been cut off by his father should be obliged to endure a meal seated next to Felicity Brightwell. She talked and flirted and made thinly veiled remarks about what she might do when she was the Viscountess St. Ashton. Tristan responded with the dry, subtly mocking banter he employed with all the women who pursued him, all the while looking down the length of the table to where his father sat with Valentine March.

He'd expected to see her at dinner. What he hadn't expected was to see her dressed in something besides that shapeless, bombazine nightmare Lady Brightwell insisted she wear. Not that Miss March was in the first stare of fashion. Not by any means. Her gown was abysmally plain and the style outdated by several years. Nevertheless, the gray silk neatly skimmed her figure, the scooped neckline showing a hint of flawless porcelain bosom, and the fitted bodice clinging to a narrow waist that, he suspected, he could easily span with both hands.

And then there was her hair.

She wore it in a loose chignon, accented with a cut glass pin. It was nothing like the padded rolls, false plaits, and jeweled combs adorning the other ladies' elaborate coiffures. And yet, Valentine March's pale golden tresses seemed to glitter in the candlelight, framing that lovely heart-shaped face that had so disconcerted him in the folly with a halo of radiant light.

An angel, Tristan thought grimly. He took a large swallow of wine, half listening to Felicity Brightwell as she chattered in his ear. For the first time, he acknowledged what had been troubling him since the moment he laid eyes on Miss March. That peculiar feeling—as if he'd just been flattened by a runaway train or struck by a bolt of lightning. That feeling with a blasted phrase attached to it. A phrase which, until earlier this afternoon, had seemed to him so damnably laughable. So utterly impossible.

Love at first sight.

The devil! He was two and thirty, not some green lad. He'd learned long ago not to mistake physical desire for something more. If only he hadn't crossed paths with Miss March today. If only it had been a month ago. Even a week ago. His heart would have remained untouched, he was sure of it.

But today he'd been blue-deviled. He'd been… Curse and confound it! He'd been *vulnerable*. And then he'd seen her. And she seemed to be everything he most needed in the world. Innocence. Truth. Beauty. All wrapped up in one angelic little package.

He took another swallow of his wine.

"Both of the cousins were sent straight back to the country in disgrace!" Miss Brightwell exclaimed with a burst of gleeful laughter. "What do you think of that, St. Ashton?"

"A very diverting tale." Tristan motioned for a footman to refill his wine.

"I should say so. It was the scandal of the season."

He glanced down the table again at his father and Miss March. They appeared to be engaged in grave conversation. If it could be called a conversation. Miss March's face was stark white and she'd hardly eaten a thing since they sat down. Every so often, he saw her nod or utter a monosyllabic reply.

What could his father be saying to her? Was he warning her to stay away from his dissolute son? Informing her that her innocence—her very status as a gentlewoman—was no protection against such an unconscionable rake?

Tristan's fingers tightened around the stem of his wine-glass in a reflexive spasm of anger.

Years ago, his father and brother had accused him of ruining a young virgin on the marriage mart. He'd denied it, of course. He'd even given his word that he'd never, nor would he ever compromise a young lady of gentle birth.

Neither had believed him.

Tristan could still remember the scathing letter John had written him. It had been filled with words like "honor" and "duty." By the time John and his father realized that the young lady was no different from any of the other adventuresses and fortune hunters who'd been pursuing Tristan since he came of age, it was too late. Tristan had broken with them, parting on the very worst of terms, and leaving London to commence a several-year stint of drunken debauchery that would have shamed the devil.

The three of them were civil now, largely as a result of Elizabeth's well-intentioned interference, but Tristan didn't think he could ever forgive John and his father for their lack of faith in him.

And if his father intended to blacken his name to Valentine March…

But that was absurd. His father would never hold up a Sinclair to public scorn. Any Sinclair. Even one as disappointing as his eldest son.

"I daresay I won't have another season next year," Miss Brightwell said. "There's no need for it. Mama thinks I'll be married by the spring. What do you say to that, St. Ashton?"

"What *can* I say, Miss Brightwell?"

"Do you have particular plans for the spring?" She gave him a secret smile. "I'll wager you do."

"And you'd be right." Tristan drank deeply from his glass. "I'll be in Northumberland."

Her brow creased. "Northumberland?"

"I have an estate there. Blackburn Priory. I'm to live there."

"Ah, a country home. But you'll be back to London for the season, won't you? You wouldn't want to be away from certain of your friends for too long."

"My dear girl, I won't be able to afford London next season, nor the season after that. I'm meant for the wilds of Northumberland, to molder away in a drafty house out in the middle of nowhere."

Miss Brightwell froze in the act of raising her water goblet to her mouth. "You're to *live* in Northumberland?"

"If one can call it living."

"And what do you mean you can't afford to reside in London? What nonsense. Everyone knows you're as rich as Croesus."

"Do they? How charming."

"To live in Northumberland all the year long? Ha!" She laughed. "Who would do so? Not you, my lord. You would die of boredom."

"Then perhaps I shall die, Miss Brightwell." Tristan finished the last of his wine and beckoned to the footman for more.

Chapter Five

By the time Valentine escaped from the other ladies in the drawing room, she felt as if she'd lived a hundred lives. Her palms were clammy. Her heart was fluttering. And her stomach was quivering like a leaf in the wind. Thank goodness for Lady Brightwell! One could always count on her to forget a glove, a handkerchief, or some other little item that would necessitate Valentine haring off all over the house in pursuit of it.

This time it was her shawl, which she was certain she'd left in the conservatory. Valentine intended to fetch it and deliver it directly to a maid. Let the maid take it back to Lady Brightwell—along with the message that her companion had retired for the evening with a blinding headache. Lady Brightwell wouldn't mind. Indeed, she'd be pleased to have so easily disposed of her companion before the gentlemen finished their port and rejoined the ladies. The Earl of Lynden's attentions hadn't gone unremarked.

"It was really not the thing to impose yourself on his lordship as you did during dinner, Miss March," she'd said to her upon entering the drawing room. "He's too much the gentleman to say so himself, but as your employer, I was quite embarrassed. I must warn you not to be so forward in future."

Under any other circumstance Valentine would have protested. She'd hardly said a word to the Earl of Lynden. This time, however, she held her tongue. There was no point in arguing with Lady Brightwell. She was too convinced of her own superiority to heed reason. And with Felicity's betrothal to St. Ashton hanging in the balance, she was poised to eliminate anyone and anything that stood in the way of her daughter becoming a viscountess.

Though how Valentine stood in the way, she had no notion. Did Lady Brightwell fear she might reveal something to Lord Lynden? But what could she reveal? That Felicity was a spoiled young miss prone to temper tantrums as severe as those of a small child?

Not that any of that had seemed to be of concern to St. Ashton. He'd laughed and flirted with Felicity all through dinner, listening with rapt attention to everything she said.

Well, let them marry. They were well suited. Both shallow and unscrupulous. Careless of the feelings of others. What did she care? She had far more important things with which to concern herself.

The most immediate of which was to find Lady Brightwell's shawl.

The Fairfords' conservatory was situated at the very back of the house. Surrounded on three sides by wide glass windows, it contained an untidy array of plants, both dead and living, and a scattering of iron benches, tables, and chairs, which had long rusted with age and neglect. Valentine entered to find the entire glass-enclosed room bathed in the soft light of a full moon. It quite took her breath away.

She stood and gazed at it for a long while as the flickering flame from the taper in her hand cast shadows over the room. A sense of peace gradually settled over her. A feeling of how very small and insignificant she was in comparison to the universe and how very trivial her problems must seem in the eyes of God.

It never failed to give her peace, staring up at the heavens. Even in her darkest moments, when all hope had seemed to be gone, she'd gazed upward and known that she hadn't been completely abandoned.

Would the moonlight look the same in India? In China? And when she stood there in a year's time, living in an exotic land surrounded by strangers, would she feel the same when she cast her eyes up to the night sky? She dearly hoped she would.

But that was many months in the future—and many months' wages yet to be saved. There was no point thinking about it now.

Recollecting herself to her task, she moved to set the candleholder down on a table, not far from a fern that had long gone brown.

"I wouldn't do that if I were you," St. Ashton said.

She gasped, her hand flying instinctively to her heart as she spun around.

He was standing in the doorway, looking tall, dark, and breathtakingly handsome. Indeed, his mere presence seemed to steal all of the oxygen from the room. "Unless you wish to burn Fairford House to the ground," he said. "Which, now I come to think of it, wouldn't be such a bad idea." He reached her in a few strides and lifted the taper from her hand.

And then he blew it out.

"Oh, now look what you've done!" she cried. "I'm meant to find Lady Brightwell's shawl!"

St. Ashton placed the candlestick on an empty iron table. "And so you can. Quite easily, I imagine." He nodded in the direction of the moon.

She followed his gaze. "It *is* very bright."

"Were I not a trifle disguised, I'd tell you it's not half as bright as your eyes or some such drivel."

"Disguised? Do you mean…you've had too much to drink?"

"Not too much. Just enough, I think."

Valentine felt him come to stand beside her, his arm touching hers. He was big and warm and disconcertingly masculine. She swallowed. "Just enough for what?"

"To follow you here to the conservatory."

She turned to find him watching her, his expression dark and brooding. "To give me back my things?" she asked faintly.

"Do you want them back?"

"Yes, of course. Do you have them with you?"

His eyes never leaving her face, he reached into his coat and pulled out the carefully folded piece of paper. He extended it to her in his hand, but as she reached out to take it, his fingers closed around the paper. "Perhaps I should keep it."

"Whatever for?"

"Because it means more to you than anything in the world," he said.

Valentine's heart commenced a heavy, almost painful thumping. "That makes no sense at all."

"It makes perfect sense to me."

"Only because you're foxed, my lord."

"Not foxed, Miss March. A trifle disguised. There's a world of difference, I assure you."

She held out her hand, palm up. "It's mine, sir. Please give it back."

"And what will you do if Miss Brightwell falls into another tantrum and throws it onto the fire? Then you'll have nothing left of your precious book of verses. Let me keep it for you, Miss March. I won't let anything happen to it, I promise you."

Valentine had the sense that something was wrong with him. Was he drunk? Was he mad? She thrust her hand closer. "I insist you give it back to me, my lord. You know I hold it very dear."

"Which is precisely why I wish to keep it."

The heavy thumping in her chest was a positive ache now. Good heavens, but he was serious! There was no hint of silky flattery or subtle seduction in his words. They were stark and raw. Brutally honest. But that couldn't be, could it? He was a practiced rake, after all. A man skilled at this sort of thing. Hadn't he confessed to following her to the conservatory?

It was as if he knew of her particular weakness. Like a predator. A predator with an injured lamb.

The very idea filled her with indignation.

"I won't allow you to make a joke of me, sir. Nor will I allow you to make sport of my feelings. Just because you—"

She broke off with a sharp intake of breath as St. Ashton caught her hand in his.

He moved his thumb over the curve of her palm and then, before she could jerk away from him, he raised her hand to his lips and brushed it with a kiss.

A quiver went through her. "My lord, you go too far," she protested. But she didn't attempt to liberate her hand. Instead she watched, wide-eyed as he kissed it once more.

"*My lord*," he repeated. "Miss March didn't I warn you to stop my lording me? My name is St. Ashton. Call me that if you must. Though, I would far prefer it if you called me Tristan."

"I'll do nothing of the sort." She extricated her hand from his grasp with one sharp tug. She was mortified to see that it was trembling. "Give me my paper and my spectacles and—"

"Ah, your spectacles. That may be a bit difficult."

"What?" She took a step away from him. "Why? You said you had them."

"And so I did. But I confess at some point this afternoon I may have succumbed to the unholy temptation to grind them under my boot heel."

Her mouth fell open.

"Your eyes *are* as bright as the moonlight, Miss March. I couldn't bear to see them hidden by those abominable spectacles for even one more moment."

"How *dared* you? You… You…" Tears sprang to her eyes. "You *unfeeling bully!*" She turned her back on him, moving to stand at the edge of the wide glass window. She was trembling with anger. But not only with anger. He'd flustered her with that kiss. He'd confused her. And he'd made her wish… made her hope…that his advances might be real. That he might actually care something for her.

Which he very obviously didn't.

Nor how could he? They'd only met for the first time that afternoon. And by his own admission he was the worst rake and reprobate of this entire wretched house party. Hadn't Mrs. Gaunt said he brought women to his bed two and three at a time?

She heard him close the distance between them. Felt his imposing presence as he once again came to stand at her side. He was silent for a long moment, as if he couldn't find the words. "Forgive me," he said at last. "I'm a damnable brute."

"Yes," she said. "You are."

His hand found hers. He pressed the folded paper into it. "Your psalm, Miss March. With my compliments."

Her fingers curled around it. "Why must you be this way?"

St. Ashton made no pretense of misunderstanding her question. "A fatal flaw in my character."

"I don't believe that."

"Don't you? After I've tormented you and bullied you and made you cry?"

She flashed him a reproving glance. "You have not succeeded in making me cry, sir."

His mouth lifted briefly in a solemn smile. "I'm glad of it."

Valentine looked at him again. "What is wrong with you? Is it… Is it something to do with your father?"

After another long pause, during which it seemed he wouldn't answer her, he motioned to an ornate iron bench near the window. She hesitated a moment before moving to sit down. St. Ashton followed, seating himself very close beside her.

"I've been cut off," he told her. "Cut off and exiled to Northumberland. I have a property there. It's isolated. Remote. I'm to live there. I daresay my father hopes I might die there."

"That can't be true."

"You think not? I've been a disappointment to him. I haven't measured up to the Sinclair standard. Indeed, according to my father, I've squandered everything that's ever been given me, including my good name. He hasn't gotten the facts entirely accurate. Not that that's ever been a barrier to his casting me as a black-hearted villain. But even if only half of what he believes were true… I won't deceive you, Miss March. I've made the devil of a mess of my life."

Valentine considered this. "The drinking and the…?"

"The gambling. The brawling. The women. Not but that I haven't given it all up these past years. God's truth, I've been living like a monk. I haven't been gaming. And I certainly haven't been brawling. I rarely even visit my club anymore. And do you know how long it's been since I've had a woman? Ah, but we mustn't discuss that topic, I see. I believe I've made you blush."

"I believe you were *trying* to make me blush," she said with a touch of asperity.

"You blush very prettily."

"What does that say to anything?"

"You need more color in your cheeks. You were too pale at dinner. Indeed, there was a moment or two I feared you'd been turned into a marble statue." He paused. "What was my father saying to you?"

Valentine flinched. "Nothing."

"Ah. Now you intrigue me. He was clearly not saying nothing." St. Ashton turned in his seat. "Was it about me? Was he warning you?"

"I beg your pardon?"

"Was he telling you that you must stay away from me?"

There was a peculiar edge to his voice. It was all of a piece with his strange demeanor this evening. Was it the drink? A reaction to the altercation with his father? She had no way of knowing for certain, but Valentine sensed that beneath St. Ashton's veneer of mocking, dry humor lay anger and bitterness and bone deep hurt. She felt a flicker of pity for him. "What an absurd idea, my lord. He didn't mention you at all."

St. Ashton raised his brows. "Not even once?"

"No, sir."

"Then what in the hell was he saying to you?"

Valentine's lips thinned into a disapproving little line. "Is it a sport for you, my lord?"

"Is what a sport?"

"To repeatedly put me out of countenance? I confess that *I* don't find it amusing. And if you persist, then I shall take my leave of you—"

He caught her arm. "Forgive me. It's not sport. If it were, trust that I wouldn't speak to you so plainly. Nor so inelegantly. That I do so is only... Good God, Miss March, can't you see that if I act the brute around you it's only the unhappy result of your putting *me* out of countenance."

She looked up at him, bewildered. "I?"

"Yes, you. Don't ask me why. I can think of one hundred reasons, most of them bad ones and none of them suitable for repeating." His fingers loosened on her forearm, his hand sliding down to hers. "If I offend you, it's not done on purpose. Pray, don't go."

Her eyes fell for an instant to where his hand covered her own. "I won't. Not yet." And quite against her will, she turned her hand, settling it more comfortably in his.

Some of the tension went out of St. Ashton's shoulders then. "Thank you."

Valentine could feel the warmth of her blush as it heated her cheeks and chest. It was impossible to appear composed in such a situation. Nevertheless, she tried. "Your father was asking about me. He asked about the village where I grew up and about my mother and father. That sort of thing."

"And you answered him."

So she had—as vaguely as possible. Not that it had put the earl off. He'd seemed to know just what to ask and just how to ask it without seeming rude or intrusive. Valentine had had no defense against such an expert technique. "Yes," she said quietly. "I answered him."

"As a result, I suppose he now knows everything about you."

"Not everything, my lord."

"He knows more about you than I do. I daresay more than I ever will."

"There's nothing worth the knowing. I was a vicar's daughter. And now I'm a lady's companion. That's all." Her heart was thumping painfully again. "I'm surprised your father would wish to stay here."

"He doesn't wish it. He's only here to prevent me from contracting what he considers to be an unsuitable marriage."

"With Felicity Brightwell?"

"Who else?"

Any secret hopes Valentine might have cherished promptly withered and died. "Yes. I see."

"He's taken it in his head that she's not good enough for me. In point of fact, he's strictly forbidden the match. He believes he can stop it somehow. And knowing him as I do, he probably can. Though, I can't see how. Especially not when he spends all of his time in conversation with you. But then my father's methods have ever been a mystery to me."

Valentine listened in numb silence. She'd always been a remarkably good listener. A quality of which Phillip Edgecombe had once taken full advantage. She'd been his friend and confidante. The person he'd come to when his cares had overwhelmed him.

"The name Edgecombe doesn't mean much around these parts anymore. Not after the way father treated everyone. And the debts! You have no idea the extent of them, Val. Mortgages on the house. Lines of credit with more banks than I can count. I mean to put it right again now he's gone, but how can I when nobody will lend me a bean?"

"Can't you just leave, Phil?" she'd asked him. *"Go somewhere else? Start over?"*

He'd given her an indulgent smile. *"And marry you? Leave Hartwood Green and traipse the globe like a pair of penniless beggars?"*

"Not beggars," she'd objected. *"Squire Pilcher mentioned a gentleman acquaintance of his with an estate in the West Country. If you were serious about going into the church—about taking orders—perhaps he might be able to arrange a living for you there."*

"It's the dearest wish of my heart," Phil had replied with seeming sincerity. *"But no. I must find a way to raise some capital, Val. When I've paid down my father's debts and have something more to offer you than my good name, then you and I shall marry. You have my word on it."*

His word. What a fool she'd been.

But that was two months ago. The morning she'd boarded the train in Surrey to the Brightwell's estate in Hertfordshire and her new life as a lady's companion, she'd vowed that she'd never again act the fool for any man. And she didn't intend to break her promise to herself now. No matter how much Lord St. Ashton might need a compassionate ear.

"If that's so, my lord," she said, "you must go join the others in the drawing room. I know Miss Brightwell is waiting for you most impatiently and—"

St. Ashton's fingers closed more firmly over her hand. "Are you so anxious to be rid of me?"

She exhaled a tremulous breath. When she spoke, her voice was equally unsteady. "Please let me go."

The sardonic humor disappeared from St. Ashton's face. "What is it? What have I said?"

"Nothing, only I still haven't found Lady Brightwell's shawl and—" She tugged at her hand. "Please. Let me find it and you may take it back with you to the drawing room."

"I'm not going back to the blasted drawing room."

"But Miss Brightwell—"

"Is that what this is about? Confound it, haven't you heard a word I've been saying to you?"

She gave another tug of her hand to no avail.

"I have no interest in Felicity Brightwell, you little idiot. And even if I did, what sort of female do you suppose would marry a penniless viscount and follow him to a moldering heap in Northumberland?"

"I would," Valentine said. The mortifying words were out before she could recall them. "If I loved someone I would follow him anywhere."

St. Ashton went still. He searched her face for a moment, his own expression stark in the glow of the moonlight. "Of course you would. You're an angel. I recognized it the first time I saw you."

She shook her head. "Don't do that. Don't make a joke of it."

"I mean it." He leaned closer to her, closer than he'd ever been before. His voice deepened. "Shall I prove it to you?"

The scent of freshly starched linen, polished leather, and lemon shaving soap rose to her nostrils. It was overwhelming to her senses. *He* was overwhelming to her sense. "N-no," she stammered.

One of his hands still retained hers, the other reached to brush a stray lock of hair from her temple. His touch was extraordinarily tender. "Let me kiss you, Valentine."

Oh, goodness.

But she couldn't allow it, could she? It would be wanton. Worse than wanton. They'd only just met today. And then there was the matter of his reputation and her own—

"Valentine," he said again.

Her name sounded wonderful murmured in his low-pitched voice. She scarcely had the heart to chastise him. "I haven't given you leave to use my Christian name, sir."

"But I must use it. And I must kiss you." He curved his hand around the back of her neck. "Just one kiss. Something to take away with me to Northumberland. Will you let me?"

His fingers were tracing a random pattern on the sensitive skin behind her ear, his breath warm against her cheek. When had he moved so close to her? "Tristan," she whispered.

It was all the encouragement he needed.

Tristan bent his head, his mouth finding hers in a brief, respectful kiss. It was the sort of kiss he had no experience with at all. Chaste. Restrained. Profoundly unsatisfying. It was over before it began.

Were he more of a gentleman he would have adhered to his word. Just one kiss, he'd said. But now, with his lips resting lightly against the voluptuous bow of hers, he couldn't stop at only one. She was too sweet, too pillow soft. His mouth moved over hers again, a featherlight touch of seductive enquiry that quickly gave way to a gentle, searching pressure. He courted her with his lips, nudging, stroking, tasting. Seeking even a flicker of response from her.

She gave it and more.

Her soft mouth yielded to his, lips parting beneath the heat of the next kiss and the next. How many kisses followed? Tristan couldn't be sure. It seemed to go on and on, one kiss dissolving into another, until her breath came as heavily as his own did. Until somehow they were no longer holding hands but fiercely embracing each other. Until he was murmuring to her nonsensically, repeating her name in a voice that ached with longing. "Valentine, Valentine."

Her arms tightened around his neck as he drew hot kisses over her jaw, her cheek, her temple. He could feel her fingers sliding through the thick locks of his hair. Could smell the faint scent of orange blossom perfume on her skin. "Tristan… we must stop."

"Once more. Please, Valentine. Let me…" He captured her lips again, kissing her as passionately as he'd ever kissed any woman before. As he lost himself in her sweetness, a shrill warning sounded somewhere in the depths of his overheated brain. She was an innocent. He had no right to handle her as he would a lover. He had no right to handle her at all. He willed his hands to remain where they were, clutching the corseted span of her trim waist, stroking the slender expanse of her back. But no power on earth could prevent the inevitable drift down to the swell of her hips and up to the lush curve of her bosom. Stroking, squeezing, caressing, while his mouth hungrily plundered hers.

He whispered something to her then. God knew what. An endearment, perhaps. Or a promise of some kind. She pressed herself against him in answer, molding her body to his chest and returning his searing kisses with a soft murmur of pleasure that set his soul aflame. "*Oh God*," he groaned. "Valentine. Let me kiss you. Let me have you. I could die tomorrow if only…"

Later he would wonder how long they'd had an audience. He'd anguish over how many had heard him moaning and begging the innocent little vicar's daughter to let him have her, as if he were a raw lad with his first woman. But now, all that registered was the sound of a high-pitched female scream, followed closely by an enormous crash as a branch of candles dropped to the floor.

"*Mama!*" Felicity Brightwell wailed at the top of her lungs.

Valentine's whole body went stiff. She tried to pull away from him, but he would not let her go. "Easy, love," he said, using his much larger frame to shield her from view of the door. "It'll be all right."

And then Lady Brightwell was there. And Lord Quinton. And—Good God!—the Earl of Lynden himself.

It was then that Tristan knew that, as far as he was concerned, things were never going to be all right again.

Chapter Six

An hour later, Tristan leaned against the library mantelpiece, his arms folded. His dark hair was disheveled and his cravat, which had been immaculate at the beginning of the evening, was now in magnificent disarray. He looked, in short, like a man who'd been interrupted in the early stages of tumbling a wench—a fact of which he was grimly aware.

Felicity Brightwell had nearly set the conservatory on fire when she dropped the candelabra held aloft in her hand. Following that, she'd nearly deafened him with her wild shrieks and sobs, all the while accusing Miss March of being a "devious little slut" and a "common harlot." It had taken her mother the better part of the hour to soothe her and then, with Lady Fairford's assistance, send her off to bed with a posset.

Now Maria Fairford sat beside Lady Brightwell, one arm around her shoulders as if to console her. Lord Lynden was seated in a chair near the fire, as ominously silent as he'd been since the moment he entered the conservatory. And Valentine…

Tristan felt an overwhelming swell of guilt as his eyes came to rest briefly on her face. She sat, pale and frighteningly white, with her hands clasped on her lap. She'd said not a word in her own defense. He very much feared she was in shock.

"Well, I will say it if no one else will," Lord Fairford proclaimed from where he stood behind his wife. He was a heavyset gentleman with thinning hair and a perpetual smile of slightly lecherous bonhomie. "If it had to happen anywhere, it's lucky it was here."

"Fairford's right," Lady Fairford agreed. "Our house parties are—" She glanced anxiously at Lord Lynden. "What I mean to say is that—"

"What m'wife means is that no one here's going to spread any gossip. Discretion is the byword at our parties. There'll be no scandal attached to this incident."

"No scandal?" Lady Brightwell moaned, a handkerchief clutched in one hand. "My daughter walked in on the man she hoped to marry in a sordid embrace with my companion! Do you think she'll ever forget the sight of it? And can you imagine she'll ever forgive me for hiring such a person? For bringing her here and allowing—"

"It would seem to me, madam, that your daughter has very little to do with the present situation," Lord Lynden said.

Tristan looked at his father in mild surprise.

"My daughter is the victim!" Lady Brightwell cried.

"If there is a victim here," Lord Lynden said, "it's Miss March."

"My companion? She's no victim of anything. She's an impudent slut who's no better than she ought to be. And I'll have her gone tonight. On the night train or the stage or a dogcart if need be. Do you hear me, Miss March? You're dismissed without reference. And without your wages, too, for you owe me the cost of those spectacles." Lady Brightwell pressed her crumpled handkerchief to her mouth. "Oh, get her out of here, Maria. I can't stand to look at her a second longer."

Tristan had had just about enough of Lady Brightwell's histrionics. "Miss March is not going anywhere," he said in a voice of perilous calm. "She's under my protection now. And anyone else who casts aspersions on her character will answer to me."

"Under your protection?" Lady Brightwell looked as if she might swoon. "Not even you, St. Ashton, would be so lost to decency as to make this…this *creature* your mistress."

"Enough." The earl rose from his chair, standing to his full, imposing height. "Fairford, I would have a moment alone with Miss March and my son."

"I can't allow that, my lord," Lady Fairford objected. "We're largely informal here, to be sure, but to leave Miss March alone with two men without the benefit of a chaperone is passing all bounds."

Lord Lynden met Valentine's eyes, and Tristan could have sworn that some silent communication passed between the two of them. "Do you wish for a chaperone?" he asked her.

"No," she whispered.

"As that may be—" Lady Fairford began, but she was silenced by her husband who moved at once to bustle the two women out of the room.

"Come, ladies," he said. "Leave them to their negotiations. Gentlemen's business, you know." Lady Brightwell declared that she must see to her daughter, and then the library doors shut and Tristan heard no more. When he looked again at Valentine, her cheeks were flaming.

"Gentlemen's business? The devil!" he swore with sudden violence. In three strides he was at her side, sinking down on his haunches in front of her and possessing himself of her two hands. "Valentine. Valentine, look at me. I have no intention of offering you a carte blanche. I mean to marry you."

Valentine gave him a look of heart-wrenching anguish. "Do you?"

"If you'll have me, yes." He squeezed her hands. "I'm a bad bet. You know that. But if you'll have me—"

"I can't marry you."

"Can't you? Why not? Because of what happened tonight? Do you fear I'm offering for you only because I've compromised you? I assure you—"

"It doesn't matter why. I can't marry you. I simply can't. I'm sorry, my lord, but you mustn't ask me anymore."

She tried to withdraw her hands, but he wouldn't allow it. He was suddenly, and quite unaccountably, angry. Never in his life had he come to the point with any lady. Never had he even considered it. And here he was, as good as on bended knee, in front of a bloody vicar's daughter and she would not have him? It beggared belief! "Why not?" he asked again. His voice was harsh. "Is it because of the money? Because I confessed to you that I have been cut off?"

"I don't care about your money."

"Then what?"

Valentine swallowed convulsively. "You said your father forbade you marrying Miss Brightwell. A baron's daughter. Trust me when I tell you that I'm a hundred times less suitable and ask me no more. If you'll…" Her eyes clouded with tears. "If you'll but lend me the money for the train to Surrey and enough for my meals along the way, I'll leave at first light and you may forget you ever met me."

"The hell I will!"

"St. Ashton." His father's voice was a low warning.

Tristan looked up from Valentine only to see his father give a stern shake of his head. That single, peremptory gesture, so typical of his high-handed sire, filled him with barely suppressed rage. He released Valentine's hands and got to his feet. He was frustrated and angry. In the grips of a painfully unfulfilled desire. But it was more than that. He was forced to admit that Valentine March's refusal hurt him.

With an effort, he summoned his familiar sardonic smile. "Well," he said dryly, "so much for gallant gestures."

His father looked at him a moment, his expression infuriatingly unreadable. And then he moved to take the chair facing Valentine. Once settled, his eyes came to rest on her face. For a long while he said nothing.

And then, to Tristan's amazement, the Earl of Lynden's stern features softened. "You look very much like your mother, my dear," he said.

Valentine exhaled slowly. Her shoulders slumped with something like defeat. "You knew her."

"Yes. I knew her."

Tristan watched the two of them with a growing sense of unease. His father had known Valentine March's mother? What the devil! He sank into the chair by the fireplace, his imagination conjuring all sorts of shocking scenarios. Suddenly, he remembered a ramshackle fellow he'd been acquainted with at Oxford. The young idiot had gone to the country for the summer and seduced a girl on his father's estate, only to later discover that the wench was one of his father's by-blows.

The memory was accompanied by a wave of nausea. Good Lord! Could Valentine March be his half-sister? He dismissed the idea as soon as it entered his mind. The Sinclair men put a recognizable stamp on their offspring. The eye color of their descendants might occasionally vary, but the hair was always black as a raven's wing.

Valentine March was far too fair to be any close relation, let alone an illegitimate half-sister.

"I asked you at dinner why you sought employment as a companion," Lord Lynden said. "You told me your father's death compelled you."

"It's the truth, my lord."

"I will ask you now what I didn't ask you then." He paused, his expression once again growing stern. "If you were in need of help, why didn't you write to Caddington Park?"

Tristan's brow furrowed at the mention of the Marquess of Stokedale's family seat in Kent. He knew Stokedale but little. He was an elegant man in his middle fifties, cold and implacable, with centuries of breeding behind him—something he let no one forget. "Why would she—?"

And then he saw it.

It was subtle, shimmering just beneath the surface, but by God it was there.

The undoubted resemblance between Valentine March and the Marquess of Stokedale.

"I did write, my lord," she said. "On two separate occasions. Lord Stokedale didn't see fit to answer me."

"Who is Stokedale to you?" Tristan asked sharply.

Valentine met his eyes from across the room. "My mother's elder brother."

Tristan swore softly, earning him a reproachful glare from his father. "Lady Sara Caddington was your mother?"

"Yes."

"Then you are—"

"Illegitimate, my lord." She brushed a tear from her cheek with an impatient flick of her hand. "Notoriously illegitimate. Now you see why marriage to me is impossible. No matter h-how badly you've compromised me."

Abruptly, Tristan stood. The action startled Valentine. She looked up at him wide-eyed, as if he might shout at her or storm from the room. But he made no move to go. Instead, he addressed his father. "Sir, I beg you would give me five minutes alone with Miss March."

His father frowned his disapproval, but he didn't object. Tristan waited in silence for him to rise from his chair, and then walked with him to the library door. He shut it firmly after him. When he turned around, he found Valentine watching him warily. He went to her, pulling up his father's vacated chair so it was facing hers. "Forgive me for not kneeling at your feet again like some heartsick young jackass," he said as he sat down. "It's late and I've had too much to drink."

"You're angry with me."

"I'm angry with myself for falling into this godawful scrape."

"It's my fault. If I hadn't allowed you to kiss me in the conservatory—"Valentine broke off. "But I daresay my behavior will be no surprise to you. Not now that you know who my mother is. It's in the blood, you see. This…this propensity for—"

"For what?"

"Wantonness," she said bitterly. Her cheeks burned with a mortified blush.

"You? Wanton?" He was sorely tempted to laugh. "My little innocent…" But he could see that she was having none of it. Who'd told her that her mother was wanton? Her father? "I didn't know your mother," he began, choosing his words with care. "I was too young. But I know of her. She's still mentioned on occasion. Shall I tell you what I've heard?"

"No."

He ignored her objection. "She was contracted from birth to wed the Duke of Carlisle. On her nineteenth birthday the betrothal was announced. Shortly after, it was discovered that she was with child. She refused to name the father—"

"Because she didn't know which of her lovers it was!"

Tristan's brows lifted. "Who the devil told you that? Your father?"

"It's the truth."

"With all due respect to the estimable vicar, it's my understanding that she knew exactly who the father was. That she refused to name him only to spare him the ignominy of being horsewhipped up and down the continent by the old marquess."

Valentine shook her head, refusing to believe it. "If that were so, why didn't he come forward and marry her? Why did he allow her to be sent away in disgrace?"

"I don't know. My own father may have some idea. He seems to know more about this affair than I realized. Indeed, I…" Tristan raked a hand through his hair, remembering his father's sudden decision to stay in Yorkshire. A decision that had come directly on the heels of his seeing Valentine in the hall. "Damn me for an idiot, I begin to think that he remained here at Fairford House because he recognized you."

"Of course he did. It's why he questioned me all through dinner. He was plainly horrified to see me mingling amongst the guests as if I were a lady of respectable birth."

"Miss March, all of London society believes that your mother was exiled to the country, where she died giving birth to her illegitimate child. By all accounts, the child died with her. The old marquess is dead. Your uncle has the title now. Who knows what really happened all those years ago?" He gentled his voice. "Whatever occurred, I can assure you, even if your mother had one hundred lovers, such things don't pass themselves down in the bloodstream. I can't explain my father's particular interest in you. Perhaps he's merely curious. Whatever the reason, I promise you that he's not so high in the instep as to refuse to dine with the illegitimate daughter of anyone."

She brushed another tear from her cheek. "How you must regret following me to the conservatory."

"There are many things I regret about this debacle, Miss March, but that's not one of them."

Her brows drew together, her eyes finding his in an uncertain question. He felt a flicker of pathetic hope. She wanted to believe him. All that was needed was a word of reassurance. A sign that he was not merely succumbing to an unpleasant duty.

"I told you the truth," he said. "I'll take that kiss with me to Northumberland. I daresay I'll live on the memory of it for a good long time." He paused, trying to summon a witty phrase or dry remark. None were forthcoming. "Must I live on the memory of it?" he asked at last. "Or will you come with me?"

"To Northumberland, do you mean?"

Tristan nodded.

"As y-your mistress?"

His jaw tightened. "I told you I have no intention of making you my mistress. I ask you to come with me as my wife or not at all."

"You father would never allow it."

"He has no say in the matter. And even if he did, I can't see why he'd object. No matter the circumstances of your mother, you came into this world the legitimate daughter of Mr. March, a vicar. Isn't that so?"

"Yes, but…"

"He married your mother and gave her his name."

"Yes. He…he said it was his Christian duty. That she'd fallen low, like Mary Magdalene, but that she'd repented and was ready to start a better life."

Tristan was beginning to suspect that the estimable vicar was a dashed loose screw. Comparing Lady Sara Caddington to Mary Magdalene? Telling Valentine that she'd inherited her mother's wantonness? No doubt there was more to the story, but now was not the time to prise it from her. "In any case," he said, "you have the vicar's name. You are Valentine March. The rest is so much ancient history."

"And yet your father recognized me. He knew who I was right away."

"I wouldn't make the mistake of comparing the wits of the general populace to those of my father. He's uncannily astute. As for those in Northumberland, there are few near Blackburn Priory who have seen a viscount, let alone anyone who would recognize the long-lost descendant of a marquess. Indeed, I expect to find the estate populated by poachers, vagrants, and criminals. We'll be lucky to have any sort of society there. Believe me, the identity of your forebears won't come up at all." He was blathering, he knew it. In truth, he couldn't remember when he'd last been so nervous. Winning her was suddenly everything.

He cleared his throat. "Now, if you have no other objections—"

"I don't know you," she said softly. "We've only just met today."

"That means nothing. Do you have any idea how many gentlemen offer for a lady after having met her only once or twice at a ball or a supper party?"

She searched his face. "But you don't wish to marry me, my lord. I don't think you wish to marry anyone. And if you did, you'd better choose an heiress. You'll need the money to repair your estate."

A hard truth, he had to admit. If he wed an heiress, perhaps he wouldn't even have to remove to Northumberland. Perhaps he could remain in London.

But as much as he hated the idea of living in rural exile at Blackburn Priory, the prospect of wedding anyone else but Valentine March was presently unthinkable. "I've spent most of my life evading women who've tried to trap me into marriage. Do you think I've ever offered for one of them before?"

"I don't know."

"The answer is no, Miss March. And after your crushing rejection to my proposal, I don't expect I'll ever have the nerve to offer for anyone again. By rejecting me, you've sentenced me to a life of lonely bachelorhood and virtually assured that the title will pass on to my infernal younger brother. I can't believe you would be so cruel."

She pressed her lips together in a reproving line. "I very much doubt your bachelorhood is a lonely one, my lord."

"And there you would be wrong."

"I also very much doubt that I'm the first female you have kissed in a conservatory."

"No. You're not the first," he admitted gravely. "But if you'll marry me, I promise that you'll be the last."

At his words, some of her resolve melted. She looked tired and confused and more than a little wistful. "You can't promise me that."

"I just have."

"It's not in your nature to be with only one woman. You told me yourself that you're a terrible rake. The worst one, you said." Her words fell to an embarrassed whisper. "I know you will grow bored with me."

"Valentine…" he began, his voice troubled.

"It's all right. I had no expectation otherwise. I only wish I hadn't made myself so ridiculous." She absently smoothed the rumpled skirts of her gown. "I'll leave in the morning, my lord, but I fear I must impose upon you for my train fare. And really, considering that you crushed my spectacles, it's not so much to ask."

"Where do you intend to go?"

"Back to Hartwood Green in Surrey. I'm sure Mrs. Pilcher will allow me stay with her until I've secured another place somewhere."

"As a lady's companion?" he asked. She nodded. "And is that how you mean to spend the rest of your life? Running and fetching shawls for henwits like Lady Brightwell?"

"Not the rest of my life. Only for another year or so. I have a plan, you see."

Something in her expression put him on his guard. "What sort of plan?"

"Well…" She clasped her hands together tightly in her lap. Her gray eyes were suddenly earnest. "I've been corresponding for some time with a lady whose husband is a member of the London Missionary Society. Perhaps you've heard of it?"

Tristan's eyes narrowed. "Go on."

"The missionaries do very important work in India and in China. And Mrs. Tennant assures me that it's quite unexceptionable for an unmarried lady to accompany—"

"Good God! That's your plan? To sail off to some heathen land with a bunch of missionaries?"

"It may sound comical to you, my lord, but—"

"Comical? It sounds bloody insane!"

In an instant she was on her feet. "I knew I shouldn't have told you!"

Tristan stood, catching her by the upper arms before she could stride toward the door. He looked down into her eyes. "Why in the hell would you want to be a missionary?"

"The usual reasons, my lord. Now if you would kindly let me go—"

"I suppose that just because you're named after a saint you feel you must go forth on some crusading mission. To what? Drive the snakes out of China and India just as St. Valentine drove them out of Ireland?"

"That was St. Patrick," she said severely. "And yes. It's what I was raised for."

"To preach to heathens in some foreign clime? To convert them into good Christians?"

She glared at him. "To help people, my lord. To show them a better way through the teachings in the Bible."

Tristan considered this. "And if you went to China or India, how many heathens do you suppose you might convert?"

"I don't know."

"A dozen? A half dozen? One?"

"I don't know!" she said again, accentuating her words with a fruitless attempt to extricate herself from his grasp. "It may be one. It may be one dozen. The number doesn't matter."

"What need have you to travel halfway round the world to reform a single godless heathen? You might do the very same staying right here in England. Indeed, you *could* do the same. With me."

Valentine stilled.

"You've already started, you know. Consider, Miss March. I've proposed to you on bended knee. I've foresworn other women. Two things I've never before done in my entire life. Two exceedingly honorable things. And that's only after having known you for a single day. Imagine what changes you might effect in a week. A month."

She shook her head in silent objection.

"I'm not making sport of you." He stepped closer, releasing his hold on her arms and moving to encircle her waist. She stiffened in alarm, but he held her in complete stillness until she began to relax against his chest. He was close. So close. He hoped to God his father would not walk in and ruin everything. "Let me do the honorable thing, Valentine," he said quietly. "Allow me to behave as a gentleman for once."

"Oh, Tristan…"

"Unless you do in fact mind living in a rundown estate in Northumberland."

She took a tremulous breath. "I don't mind it."

He bowed his head until his forehead rested lightly against hers. "Unless you mind marrying a gentleman with a reputation as black as mine."

"I do not mind it. As long as you promise—"

"I promise," he said huskily. "I'll do better, Valentine. I'll change. You do believe people can change, don't you?"

"Yes," she whispered.

"Then let me do the honorable thing."

"Very well."

Tristan closed his eyes briefly against a staggering swell of relief. "Is that a yes?"

"Yes," she said. "Yes, Tristan. I will marry you."

Chapter Seven

The next morning Valentine was awakened by the sound of two giggling maids outside her bedroom door. She couldn't hear what they were saying. Nor did she need to. It was clear that the events of last night hadn't been quietly hushed up. Indeed, she expected that the whole house was bubbling with gossip, from the master and mistress all the way down to the lowest scullery maid. She was tempted to pull her pillow over her head and go back to sleep, but a scratch at the door, followed immediately by the entry of one of the very same giggling maids, necessitated that she rise and begin a hurried toilette.

Tristan had sent word that she was to meet him for a morning drive. It sounded more of a summons than a request. As Valentine washed with ice-cold water and combed the tangles from her long hair, she wondered if he intended to tell her that he'd changed his mind. Not but that he hadn't seemed sincere enough in his declarations last night. More than sincere, if she was honest. His promises to her had been in the manner of a solemn vow. However, she was swiftly coming to understand that the Viscount St. Ashton was a wildly impulsive gentleman. The sort of gentleman used to indulging his every whim—whether following a vulnerable lady's companion to a conservatory or crushing a pair of spectacles under his boot heel.

And then there was the unfortunate fact that last night he'd been half-drunk or a trifle disguised, or whatever he'd called it. The cold light of dawn had likely brought sober common sense with it. He must realize now that he hadn't needed to propose marriage at all.

He'd compromised her, true enough, but she was nothing but a lady's companion. Only a step up from the silly parlor maids who sighed and swooned in Tristan's wake, really. He would no doubt inform her that, upon reflection, he'd decided it would be best that she simply return to Surrey.

Though why he must take her for a drive in order to do it, she had no idea.

After pinning up her hair, she dressed quickly in an ill-fitting gown and knee-length wool mantle, buttoning the latter all the way up to her neck. It was early enough that she didn't need to worry about running into Lady Brightwell or Felicity. They didn't rise from bed until well past ten. Even so, as she ducked out of her third floor room and hurried down the stairs, she felt an overwhelming sense of urgency. Being called a devious slut and a common harlot had been a thoroughly unpleasant experience. One she didn't care to repeat anytime soon.

Not that the name-calling had been the worst of it. There had first been the mortification of being caught in a compromising position with a known rake. And then the frank conversation about her mother and the ignominious circumstances of her birth. Either one of which would have been enough to render last evening one of the worst nights of her entire life.

And yet, amongst all the humiliation, there were moments she knew she'd hold close to her heart forever. Tristan's low-pitched voice as he begged her to let him do the honorable thing.

And that kiss.

That scorching, all-consuming kiss.

It had ignited something in her. Something wanton, she'd thought later. But in the moment, it had been wonderful. Beautiful. Was it how he kissed all his women? A lowering thought!

She descended the final flight of stairs to find Tristan pacing in the front hall. His thick black hair was disheveled, his face shadowed and grim. If it were not for the immaculate state of his clothes, she might have suspected that he'd been up all night. As it was, his black cravat was neatly tied and his top boots polished to a mirror shine. His caped greatcoat succeeded in making him appear altogether larger and far more intimidating than he already was.

When he caught sight of her, he frowned. "Miss March," he said, sounding as cross as he looked.

"My lord." She ignored his irritation, focusing instead on retying the wayward strings of her bonnet. Her gloved fingers were awkward and clumsy, refusing to cooperate. And no wonder. Her heart was thumping so heavily she thought she might expire.

He'd changed his mind.

It was as plain as anything.

She told herself that she should be relieved, but as she followed Tristan out to the drive, she felt an all too familiar weight descend upon her. Such a feeling had been her almost constant companion since the death of her father. When she accepted Tristan's proposal, she'd begun to believe, for just a moment, that she would once again have a proper place in the world. That she would no longer be alone. More fool her! She should have known that marriage wouldn't be the answer to her troubles. Especially not a marriage to a gentleman like the Viscount St. Ashton.

"We'll be lucky if the wheels don't fall off," Tristan muttered as he handed her up into the curricle.

Valentine cast an absent glance at the rickety vehicle. It was attached to two very fine-looking chestnuts, which succeeded in making it appear even shabbier by comparison. "To whom does it belong?"

Tristan vaulted up into the carriage seat beside her and gathered the reins. "The curricle belongs to Fairford. The horses belong to me." He shouted at the groom to release their heads and gave the horses the office to start. They leapt forward in their traces, causing Valentine to clutch nervously at the side of her seat.

"I left my own curricle behind in London," he explained, his eyes straight ahead on the road. "I didn't plan to do any driving here in Yorkshire."

She inhaled a breath of cold air. It was a frosty morning, the fog sitting heavily on the hills. It didn't look like it would rain, but one never knew. "You needn't have bothered taking me for a drive."

"No?"

"If you have something you wish to tell me, you might just as easily have said it in the library."

"I've spent the better part of the night in Fairford's library. If I never see it again, it will be too soon."

Valentine was aware that he'd stayed in the library in order to speak privately with his father. She hadn't remained for that conversation. Indeed, as soon as Tristan had received her acceptance to his proposal, he'd compelled her to go to bed and she'd been more than willing to oblige him. As he'd escorted her from the room, all traces of dry humor in his expression had been gone. In their place was a grim strength of purpose. As if he were about to fight a duel—or face a firing squad.

"The better part of the night?" she echoed faintly. "Doing what?"

"Talking with my father."

"Oh." She could think of nothing else to say. Had Lord Lynden convinced him of the unsuitability of the match? It certainly sounded that way.

Valentine stared numbly at the passing scenery. She didn't know how many minutes passed in silence. Not that Tristan appeared to mind the lack of conversation. The horses were going at a remarkably quick clip and he was addressing himself solely to the task of driving them.

When they reached the end of the long drive, she expected him to turn left through a bank of trees at the edge of the estate. Instead, he guided the horses out onto the main road.

She looked up at him in vague alarm. "I thought you were taking me for a drive around the park?"

"Whatever gave you that idea?"

"It seemed a reasonable guess." She sat up taller in her seat, craning to see ahead. "Where *are* we going?"

"To York."

"*What?*"

"York, Miss March. The nearest town in this godforsaken wilderness."

"I can't drive with you to York!"

"Why not? We're in an open carriage. It's all perfectly respectable."

"Perhaps it would be if we were merely taking a turn about the grounds, but to drive all the way to York? Why, it's nearly fifteen miles away!"

"A negligible distance for my cattle. I daresay we'll get there in an hour and a half. Perhaps sooner, depending on the quality of the roads—and providing this curricle doesn't disintegrate beneath us. In any case, it'll give us time to discuss a few matters. I trust you're warm enough?"

"Yes, but—" She broke off as it suddenly occurred to her what the purpose of their journey was. There was a railway station in York, wasn't there? He was driving her there to put her on the train. Getting rid of her before anyone else had risen for the day. As if she were some distasteful secret that must be disposed of.

She turned her head away from him, once again staring in the opposite direction. Her hand clenched tightly on the seat. "You might have at least allowed me to pack my things," she said.

Tristan glanced at her. "What things?"

"My clothes. My comb. My toothpowder. It may seem like nothing to you, but—"

"Your clothes should be consigned to the dustbin," he said matter-of-factly. "Never in my life have I seen a collection of garments so unflattering." He deftly maneuvered the horses past a slow-moving coach. "Indeed, Miss March, I can safely say that you are the least fashionable female I've ever had the misfortune to take driving."

A mortified blush rose in her cheeks. "As I said before, sir, you needn't have taken me driving at all."

"It's a necessary journey," he said. "York is not Paris or London, I know. But I daresay we might find a dressmaker there to run you up a few gowns. The rest we'll purchase at some shop or other." He cast her another frowning glance. "Are you sure you're warm enough?"

Valentine stared at him in blank astonishment. "Do you mean…you're taking me to York to buy me *clothes*?"

"Amongst other things."

"But you must know that I can't accept gifts from you, my lord! It would be wholly improper for me to—"

"Not in the least. A gentleman is expected to lavish gifts on his betrothed. And it's quite unexceptional for his betrothed to accept them."

She took a deep breath. "*Are* we still betrothed then?"

He scowled at her. "What sort of question is that?"

"I thought you'd changed your mind." His scowled deepened, but she continued in a rush. "You seemed to be in a terribly bad mood when I came downstairs. And you said you'd been up all night with your father so I assumed he'd persuaded you what a mistake it would be for us to marry. And now, for you to drive me to York, where the train comes through and—"

"Is this what's been occupying your mind since we left Fairford House?"

"I'm afraid so."

"Even though last night I solemnly promised you—"

"I know. And I don't mean to insult you by doubting your word. But you must understand the difficulty of my position. I don't know what went on when you spoke to your father. I don't know what's going to happen next. I've lost my job and Lady Brightwell has withheld my wages. I'm completely at the mercy of others. If anything should happen... If you should change your mind..."

Her voice trailed off as Tristan eased the horses to the side of the road and brought the curricle to a halt. He set the brake and turned to face her, the expression in his eyes hard to read.

"I haven't changed my mind," he said.

"Haven't you?" she asked faintly.

"No."

"Then why—?"

"If I'm cross today it's simply because the interview with my father last night was profoundly unpleasant. You see, Miss

March, in addition to reading me a lecture on my lack of morals and my lack of honor, he informed me in no uncertain terms what's to be done about you."

"About *me?*"

"I intended to discuss it with you on the return journey from York."

Valentine bristled. The very idea of two gentlemen making decisions about what was to be done with her! As if she had no will or mind of her own. "We'll discuss it now, if you please."

Tristan looked at her for several moments. "As you wish."

She waited, becoming more and more anxious the longer it took him to come to the point.

"According to my father, there are only two acceptable solutions to our present dilemma. The first, and the one he favors, would result in our not marrying."

Her heart plummeted. "Go on."

"My father proposes that he pay a visit to the Marquess of Stokedale on your behalf. Failing that, he says there are any number of Caddington relations scattered about who might be willing to take you in once they know that you're Lady Sara's daughter."

"Is that true?" she asked, suppressing a pathetic flare of hope. "There really might be relatives of my mother who would *want* me?"

"It's possible, yes. Though God knows how long it would take to find them."

"And what would happen to me in the meantime? Would I go back to Hartwood Green? To Mrs. Pilcher?"

"No. My father would send you to Devonshire to stay with my brother and his wife. You would be safe enough there until something is sorted out with Stokedale or the Caddingtons."

Her palms felt damp within her gloves. She pressed them flat on her lap. "And then you and I wouldn't marry at all."

"No. We would not." He hesitated briefly before adding, "In time, my father believes the Caddingtons would find you a more appropriate husband."

"More appropriate to my station, I suppose he means."

"He means that they would find you a husband who's not a hardened, conscienceless rake. A husband who can be relied on to protect you and provide for you. A husband, in short, who is not me."

Valentine lifted her gaze to his face. She thought she heard a flicker of bitterness in his voice. Or perhaps even anger. But when she met his eyes, there was nothing there except the same frustratingly unreadable expression. "You said there were two options," she reminded him.

"So there are."

"Well?"

"In the second scenario, we would marry," he said. "But it would be a very long engagement. A year, at least. During which you would be sent to Devonshire to stay with my brother and his wife and I would go to Northumberland. Once Blackburn Priory is both habitable and profitable, you and I would be married at St. George's, Hanover Square. Everything respectable and above board with no hint of scandal. As befits the Earl of Lynden's heir."

The idea of a grand wedding at St. George's, Hanover Square left Valentine cold. And it surely couldn't be a wise idea. Why, at such a venue all of society would likely be in attendance. All of them come to see the Viscount St. Ashton wed the bastard daughter of the infamous Lady Sara Caddington. How could the earl even consider such a thing? Unless…

"Such a long engagement," she said. "It's almost as if he's hoping that, given enough time, you'll change your mind."

"On the contrary. The long engagement is for your protection, not mine." He paused, his jaw tightening. "If you must know, my father expects me to behave dishonorably. To abandon my duties to Blackburn Priory. Fall into vice again or become enamored of some tart in a tavern and end up chasing her halfway to France. He reasons that it's better such things happen during a long engagement—while you're still free to extricate yourself from my clutches."

This time the underlying bitterness and anger in his voice were unmistakable. What had the earl said to him last night? Whatever it was, it had hurt him. And he *was* capable of being hurt, of that she had no doubt. "Your father's concerns seem to be very specific," she said carefully. "Have you ever done any of those things before? Followed a…a female…halfway to France, I mean."

"Years ago. Though I didn't follow anyone anywhere. I left England with a mistress. But she was an actress, not a tavern wench. And it was Ireland, not France."

Valentine opened her mouth only to promptly close it again. She wouldn't demean herself by enquiring whether this actress was still his mistress, no matter how much she wished to know. "In each scenario I'm to go and live with your brother and his wife," she said instead. "Yet I can't imagine they're so keen to have a complete stranger come to stay. And certainly not for a year or more."

"Probably not. But my sister-in-law, Elizabeth, would make you welcome enough. They have a great deal of room there. You'd be in no one's way. And they are annoyingly respectable. There would be no more risks to your reputation. No more gentleman deviling you in conservatories."

"And this is what your father wishes for me," she mused. "I don't understand why he would put himself to the trouble."

"I believe he feels somewhat protective of you. He hasn't said why, but knowing him and his dashed sense of honor, I imagine he sees himself as righting some long-ago wrong done to your mother. You must know that there aren't many who agreed with the way the old marquess handled things."

A wrong done to her mother? She wasn't used to looking at the situation in such a way. Especially when Papa had always presented the opposite view. According to him, her mother had been entirely at fault. "After Papa died, I wrote to the Marquess of Stokedale twice."

"Did you?"

"Yes. I told him I was alone in the world now. That I had no one else to turn to. I asked for his help." She grimaced at the memory. "How I despised myself for writing those letters! I wouldn't have done it except that Phil told me—"

"*Phil?*" Tristan interrupted sharply.

"Phillip Edgecombe. A gentleman from my village in Surrey."

"An elderly friend of your fathers, I presume? A dodder-ing septuagenarian who's half blind and walks with the aid of two sticks?"

She sensed he was being sarcastic, but couldn't for the life of her fathom why. "Mr. Edgecombe is all of eight and twenty, my lord. And he's in perfect health. At least, he was when last I saw him."

"Who is he?"

"I've just told you—"

"Who is he to *you*?"

"Oh. I see." Her brow furrowed. "Well…if you must know…Mr. Edgecombe and I had a sort of understanding."

"An *understanding*?"

"There's no need to bellow at me, sir."

"Was I bellowing? I do beg your pardon." This time his sarcasm was unmistakable. "Please continue, Miss March."

"Yes, well…we *had* an understanding, but nothing was ever formally announced. The fact is, Phil—Mr. Edgecombe, I mean—never had any intention of marrying me."

"It was Edgecombe who pressed you to write to the Mar-quess of Stokedale," Tristan said. It was not a question.

"Yes."

"I suppose he thought there was a chance you might be in line for some of the Caddington fortune."

"He never said so. But when the first letter went unan-swered, he urged me to write again. For my own benefit, he said. Because they were my family and I shouldn't be all alone. It was only when the second letter received no reply that he told me we couldn't marry. Though he did say he would always love me and would forever be my friend."

"He sounds like an unmitigated ass."

Valentine felt the smallest thrill of pleasure at Tristan's unkind remark. "As to that—"

"Did you love him?" he asked.

She exhaled a slow breath. "No. At least, not in the way I think you mean. He was my friend. I've known him most of my life, you see. But I realize now that no friend would ever have asked me to write those letters. To humble myself in such a way—and to such a man." She gave a short, choked laugh. "Well, what does it matter now? I daresay the Marquess of Stokedale didn't even read them."

"Stokedale is very like his father was before him. Cold. Inflexible. Too proud for his own good."

"Well, I don't ever wish to meet him," Valentine declared. "And I won't accept his help, even if your father persuades him to give it to me. I'd rather go to a workhouse. I'd rather starve."

"Ah. The famous Caddington pride."

"It's not pride! It's self-respect. Besides," she added stiffly, "I'm nothing like them."

"No? Then I suppose I must beg your pardon again."

She sighed. "Perhaps it is a Caddington trait. If so, I can't help it. But I'd never be cold or inflexible." Something in Tristan's face brought an immediate flush to her own. Was he thinking of their kiss? She'd certainly not been cold and inflexible then. "What I mean to say is that I'd never be unjust or unforgiving. Especially not to a person who's in their present predicament through no fault of their own."

"I begin to think that the first option is not to your liking."

"The first option…? Oh, yes. I see."

"That leaves the second option. The one that culminates with you marrying me."

"At St. George's, Hanover Square." She frowned.

"You don't care for St. George's?" He frowned as well. "I confess, neither do I. In any case, we have a year or more to accustom ourselves to the idea."

A year or more in which she would live with strangers who didn't want her. Would it be so different from being a lady's companion? Or a governess? Yes, she thought miserably. At least as a paid employee there would be clear expectations. There would be rules. As an unwanted guest, she would be there on sufferance. Never knowing from one moment to the next what she should be doing or not doing. And all the while feeling the full weight of her obligation. "Do you mind a long engagement?" she asked him.

"Of course I mind it."

"I suppose it would give us time to get to know each other better."

He raised a brow. "With me in Northumberland?"

"We could write to each other. Many friendships develop through correspondence. Romances, too. Just look at Héloïse and Abélard."

"A touching love story. I believe at the close of it Abélard was castrated."

Her face reddened. "That was only one small part of the tale," she said in her most reproving tone.

"One small part? My little innocent, trust me when I tell you that big or small has nothing to do with it. Once a fellow has been castrated, the story is over."

She pressed her hands to her burning cheeks. She hadn't known it was possible to blush so deeply. "You are awful."

Strangely enough, this made him grin. It was the first sign of genuine good humor she'd seen in him all morning. "Completely awful," he agreed. He gathered up the reins and, with a touch of the whip, urged the horses forward in their traces, guiding them expertly back onto the road. "We have some time before we arrive in York. You may recite an improving psalm to me if you like."

"A psalm about the fate that awaits men who say scandalous things to ladies?"

"Is there such a psalm?"

Valentine racked her brain for some passage in the Bible that she might employ as a set-down, only to be immediately overcome with guilt that she'd consider using the Bible for such an unkind purpose. "No," she said, chastened. "There's not."

He cast her a measuring sidelong glance. "Very well then, recite the rest of that verse from the paper you had with you in the folly. I'll start, shall I? 'Arise, my love, my fair one and come away with me…to York.'"

It was all she could do to repress a completely inappropriate gurgle of laughter. "You *would* make a joke of the Bible."

But Tristan must have seen her lips quiver, for he was at once remarkably cheerful and very like he'd been before the unfortunate incident in the conservatory. "Come now, Miss March. You must give me credit for remembering the first lines. Now you recite the rest. I'll direct my attention to memorizing. And, with any luck, by the time we return to Fairford House, you'll have made a Biblical scholar out of me."

Chapter Eight

The hours spent in York with Valentine March were some of the happiest moments in Tristan's recent memory. He wasn't accustomed to squiring a gently bred lady about town. He'd never properly courted anyone, nor had he troubled himself with playing the attentive admirer. His past visits to dressmakers, milliners, and jewelers had always been on behalf of some mistress or other. But Valentine March was no pampered courtesan accepting his gifts as just one of the many perks of her carnal employment. Valentine was a lady. More importantly, she was *his* lady.

From the moment he lifted her down from the curricle, she'd set her hand on his arm and, for the bulk of the day, she hadn't removed it. At times, he found himself covering that hand protectively with his own and more than one passing gentleman who admired her for a second too long was the recipient of his thunderous scowl.

He took her first to a small dress shop off Bridge Street that he'd heard Mrs. Ravenscroft mention the previous night at dinner. It was a respectable establishment run by a very competent modiste. Madame Gerrard, as she introduced herself, fluttered about Valentine, examining her face and figure with a critical eye. As she murmured appreciatively in English accented French, Valentine informed her that she would need only three gowns—two for day and one for evening.

Madame said nothing, merely summoned two assistant seamstresses who instantly appeared and, after a brief exchange with their employer, whisked Valentine into the back room where she was to be stripped and measured.

"Three gowns, Monsieur?" Madame Gerrard asked. She shook her head, clucking her tongue in disapproval. "A shame! She is a beautiful lady. So fair. And with such a shape!"

Tristan didn't need to be reminded. "She'll need more than three gowns, obviously."

Madame's dark eyes became shrewd. "How many more?"

"As many gowns as can be made ready today," he said. "And everything that goes with them."

"*Everything*, Monsieur?"

"Everything," he repeated emphatically.

Everything, it turned out, comprised corsets, crinolines, petticoats, stockings, shoes, bonnets, and gloves. Most were available through Madame Gerrard. The remainder, Madame informed him, must be purchased from the local draper and milliner. Tristan had a feeling Valentine would balk at additional shopping and, for an extortionate sum, persuaded the modiste to send out some of her girls to bring back the requisite items to the shop.

Meanwhile, he established himself in one of the tastefully upholstered chairs in the corner of the showroom, prepared to wait however many hours it took. With his mistresses, he'd invariably taken himself off somewhere for a drink—either that or been invited into the backroom to watch the fitting—but with Valentine he was determined to be both respectful and attentive. Besides, she had no maid with her and he refused to leave her unprotected. Anything could happen.

Though, at the moment, there was a greater likelihood of her bolting for freedom than of some random man accosting her.

He'd seen the look in her eyes as he informed her of the earl's proposed solutions to their current dilemma. He could tell that the options were as unappealing to her as they had been to him. She didn't want to go to London and marry at St. George's, Hanover Square any more than she wanted to spend a prolonged period of time with John and Elizabeth in Devonshire. In truth, he wasn't entirely sure what she wanted.

But she'd responded to his embrace last night with enough passion to set off all the fireworks at Cremorne Gardens. She'd kissed him and clung to him. She'd promised to marry him.

And in return he'd promised her that he would do better. That he would change.

Good Lord, but she'd believed him.

She'd believed him.

Knowing that, how in the world was he ever supposed to let her go?

Tristan folded his arms and settled farther back into the chair. He watched the shop assistants dart in and out of the back room with pattern books, ribbons, and bolts of fabric, trying his damnedest not to imagine Valentine standing only a few yards away in nothing but her shift.

All the things his father had said to him during that excruciating lecture in the library last night were true. His manners *were* execrable. His language *did* belong in the gutter. And he *had* handled Valentine March like a tavern doxy instead of a gently bred vicar's daughter.

His father had definite ideas about how his heir should conduct himself now that he was at last contemplating marriage to a respectable young lady. According to the earl, he was, above all, to control his baser urges and address himself to his future wife—whomever she might be—with no more than respectful affection. Tristan had a grim idea of what that entailed. He was well acquainted with the sort of bloodless unions entered into by many of his peers. Respectful affection was composed of no more than civil dialogue, polite but restrained flirtation, and dutiful couplings under cover of darkness until at least two sons were produced to secure the line.

Is that how the Earl of Lynden had conducted his own marriage? Tristan couldn't remember. He'd barely been two years old when his mother died. Except for a vague recollection of the scent of powder and lavender that had lingered on her soft white skin, he had no memory of her at all.

The portrait of her at Lyndwood Hall showed her as a graceful dark-haired woman dripping in jewels. As a boy, he'd gone up to the picture gallery more times than he could count and sat cross-legged on the floor in the front of that painting. His mother's blue eyes, so similar to those of his brother John, had seemed to look down on him, her face lit with a benevolent, maternal glow. Like a Madonna, he once told his father. But at the mention of the late countess, the earl's expression had hardened into a cold, impenetrable mask. And that was something of his childhood that Tristan *did* remember. That cold, remote look that had come into his father's eyes in the years following his mother's death. The years during which the earl had only seemed to smile when he was in the presence of his younger son.

He'd loved her. Loved her enough that it had been over a decade before he took a mistress. And yet, the earl had no such expectation for his heir. Tristan was to be consigned to a marriage in which he must always keep himself under rigid control. Not that he didn't appreciate his father's reasoning. The first time he'd had Valentine alone he'd bullied her. The second, he'd forced himself on her. And only this morning he'd brought up the subject of castration, of all things. What the devil had he been thinking?

But he knew exactly what he'd been thinking. He'd been thinking that she was blue-deviled about what had happened the night before. That she was anxious about the future. That he would do anything—say anything—to distract her. Not that his motives had been entirely altruistic. He'd wanted to make her blush. He'd wanted to see her gray eyes flash with righteous outrage. To hear one of her prim little sermons.

He was beginning to suspect that a brief, dutiful coupling with his future viscountess was not going to be nearly enough.

At half past one, Valentine emerged from the backroom clothed in a white muslin Garibaldi blouse paired with a skirt made of vibrant emerald-green silk. The color emphasized the flawless porcelain of her skin and the elegant silhouette—complete with a slim velvet belt and delicate gilt buckle—set off her neat little figure to magnificent effect. In her hand she held a straw spoon bonnet trimmed in green silk ribbons and a profusion of artificial flowers and lace. She was eyeing it dubiously as she approached him.

"May I speak with you?" she asked.

Tristan's gaze roved over her, his mouth suddenly dry. "If you wish." He motioned to the front of the shop, out of hearing range of Madame Gerrard and her assistants. "I take it that you don't like that hat."

"I do like it. Very much. Indeed, I like everything very much. Especially this beautiful skirt. But—"

"You look very becoming," he said.

"Oh? Do you really think so?" She smoothed her silk skirts with an almost reverent touch, her objections temporarily forgotten. "It has a matching Zouave jacket. Madame Gerrard was making it up for another lady who's near to my size. She's given it to me along with some of the other lady's gowns. It doesn't seem very fair. To the other lady, I mean. But Madame Gerrard says this sort of thing is done all the time."

"Madame Gerrard is right."

"Still"—she sank her voice even lower—"I think it must all be very expensive."

"What does that signify?"

"It's too much, my lord."

"It's merely a few frocks, Miss March. Far less costly than outfitting a female for the season in London. In any event, I'm not yet a bankrupt."

"Even so, you must conserve all your resources for Blackburn Priory, mustn't you? And I could easily make do with half as many gowns or less." Again, her voice fell to a whisper. "Not to mention that I hardly need so many pairs of stockings. And surely they needn't all be silk? As for these new bonnets…" She looked down at the rather frivolous confection in her hand. "They're far too fine. Indeed, my lord, I cannot accept them."

Tristan wished to God she hadn't mentioned her silk stockings. Damnation, did she think he was made of stone? "If there's something you truly don't like, I won't compel you to keep it, but as far as cutting the order in half, the answer is no. As we've already discussed, it's my right as your betrothed to buy you whatever I wish. And I might well add, Miss March, that it's now your duty to dress in a manner befitting the next Viscountess St. Ashton."

She was clutching her bonnet in both hands now, her brows drawn together in an anxious line. "You know there's every chance we won't marry at all."

He went very still. "Have you made a decision, then?"

"No, but—"

"Very well. Until you do, I'll continue to act as your betrothed." With that, he informed the modiste that they'd return in two hours for the rest of their order and, after directing Valentine to put on her new bonnet, ushered her out the front door of the dress shop.

"Return in two hours from where?" Valentine asked as she took his proffered arm.

"Are you hungry?"

"Famished," she admitted.

Tristan placed his hand over hers. "There's an inn up ahead. I'll bespeak a private parlor for us and we can have something to eat." He smiled down at her. "Perhaps, if you're very well-behaved, I'll even allow you to have a sip of my ale."

By the time they returned to Fairford House, the sun was sinking behind the hills. Tristan stopped the curricle at the front steps and leapt down from his seat. A stable lad ran up to hold the horses' heads and a young footman—the same, impudent fellow who had importuned Valentine the previous day—emerged to take charge of her packages.

Valentine watched Tristan as he strode round to her side of the carriage. He looked different to her now. Less remote and coldly aristocrat. Indeed, after spending the better part of the day with him, he seemed much more than just a handsome rake. He'd teased her and made her laugh the entire journey home. He'd been kind and solicitous, too. At luncheon, he'd peeled and sectioned an orange for her. And he'd offered her not one but several sips of his ale.

She hadn't once felt as if he were attempting to seduce her or take advantage. Quite the opposite, in fact. He'd been protective toward her. Rather like she imagined an elder brother might be.

A small part of her owned to being slightly disappointed. Every time he touched her, she felt dozens of butterflies unfurl their wings in her stomach. Her pulse skipped and her palms dampened, the memory of his kisses and his powerful embrace making her a veritable puddle of silly, wilting femininity. Tristan, by contrast, seemed totally unaffected. Even when he quizzed her about some indecent thing or other, he managed to do so in a manner that was far more humorous than lecherous.

She caught up the bulk of her emerald-green silk skirts in her hand. They stood out wide from her body over a profusion of petticoats and a stiff horsehair crinoline. Thank goodness she hadn't heeded Madame Gerrard's advice about purchasing one of the newer varieties of cage crinoline. Made of hooped wires and fabric tape, it was a style favored by Lady Brightwell and her daughter—a style which made one's skirts balloon out to the point of caricature. As it was, Valentine could scarcely turn in the seat of the curricle with so much fabric spilling all about her.

Tristan gave her a slight smile as he reached up to catch her around the waist, lifting her out of the curricle and setting her feet down gently onto the paving stones. His large hands lingered a moment on the swell of her hips.

He gazed down at her and she met his eyes, venturing a shy smile of her own. She could feel the warmth blooming in her cheeks. "What happens now?" she asked.

"Now?" He dropped his hands, taking a step away from her. "I recommend a bath and a change of clothes. It's impossible to travel in an open carriage without being covered all over with grime."

Valentine's smile faded. Last night he had called her an angel and begged her to let him have her, but she was beginning to think that his sweet words and actions the previous evening owed more to excessive drink than any particular passion he may have felt for her. "And after that?"

His expression grew somber. "Then we talk."

The footman cleared his throat. "Beg pardon, my lord. Shall I take these parcels to your rooms?"

Valentine hurried forward. "I'll take them." She lifted the stack of white ribbon-tied boxes from the footman's arms. She was thankful that neither the footman nor Tristan knew what was in them. At least, she didn't think that Tristan knew. Then again, a practiced rake might well realize that boxes of a certain size could only contain a woman's underthings.

She glanced at Tristan. "If you'll excuse me, my lord."

Tristan bowed. "Miss March."

Ignoring the footman's impertinent stare, she turned and ran up the front steps into the house. The main hall was empty; however, she could hear ribald laughter rippling out from the direction of the conservatory. A jolt of alarm quickened her pace. She'd seen none of Lord and Lady Fairford's guests since last night.

Nor did she wish to.

She bounded up the stairs to her third floor bedroom, the stack of boxes in her arms and her heavy skirts clutched in one hand. Tristan hadn't followed her into the house. She suspected he'd stayed behind to lecture the stable lad about how to care for his horses or some such thing. Not that it mattered. He'd made it plain that he had no desire to talk at the moment.

It was frustrating, really. Nothing had been settled between them during their trip to York. If anything, she had even more questions.

And even more doubts.

What had she been thinking to allow him to buy her so many beautiful things? Good gracious, he must have spent a small fortune! She should have refused him outright. Insisted that her own gowns were quite good enough, thank you very much.

But he hadn't approved of her clothing. It was a poor reflection on him, he'd said. Or something to that effect.

She steadied her stack of boxes beneath her chin, freeing her right hand to twist the doorknob to her bedroom. The door swung open. She stepped inside, poised to drop her packages onto the bed, only to come to an abrupt and very startled halt.

"Well, well." Felicity Brightwell was standing with her back to the wooden chest-of-drawers in the corner. Behind her, two drawers stood open, their meager contents spilling out. "You've returned at last."

Valentine's took in the scene before her in one comprehensive glance. "Have you been rifling through my things?"

"What things? Your darned stockings? Your threadbare undergarments?" She cast a poisonous look at the packages in Valentine's arms before sweeping her with the same, contemptuous glare from the top of her spoon bonnet to the hem of her emerald-green skirts. "I see that St. Ashton is attempting to make a silk purse from a sow's ear. You may tell him for me that he's failed miserably."

Valentine deposited her boxes on the edge of the bed and proceeded to untie the wide silk ribbons of her new bonnet. She was amazed at the steadiness of her hands. "You have no right to go through my things. Nor to be in my room."

"I've been waiting for you," Felicity replied.

"To what purpose?"

"So that we might speak in private."

Valentine placed her bonnet on the bed along with her packages. She'd hoped to avoid any more unpleasantness with Lady Brightwell and her daughter. "I can't imagine we have anything useful to say to each other."

"I don't care what *you* have to say." Felicity's voice rose in volume with every word. "But *I* am determined to speak my mind."

Valentine moved to shut the door to her room. Unless she was very much mistaken, Felicity Brightwell was about to subject her to an outpouring of vitriol and she'd much rather the servants not hear it. They'd already heard quite enough last night. "Speak if you must. And then go."

Felicity's face flushed with anger. "You wouldn't have dared use such a tone with me yesterday."

"Yesterday I was still your mother's companion."

"And today you aren't, is that it? She's let you go without a reference—and without your last month's wages, too."

"She has."

"Because you're a slut who's no better than she ought to be."

Valentine leaned back against the closed door, her hands clasped loosely at her waist. Her heart was beating swift as a hummingbird's. She despised confrontations. "Such vulgarity does you no credit."

Felicity snorted. "They're Mama's words, not mine. She says you and St. Ashton have come to some sort of sordid arrangement." She walked alongside the bed, giving the packages an angry flick with her hand. The topmost box toppled to the floor. "Did he give you all of these things?"

Valentine's gaze dropped briefly to the smallish package on the ground. It contained five pairs of silk stockings in shades of black, white, pink, cream, and gray. The sixth pair was currently on her legs, as fine as cobwebs, secured above her knees with a new pair of embroidered French garters. She raised her eyes back to Felicity's face. The knowing expression she found there provoked a sudden twinge of shame.

A sordid arrangement.

Is that what it was? Something sordid?

She cataloged the events of the past night in her mind.

An infamous rake had embraced her. Kissed her. And she'd succumbed to his advances with an appalling display of eagerness. Not only succumbed. She'd returned his kisses in full measure.

Because he'd talked to her as if she were a real person and not a servant. Because he'd shown her kindness and affection—two things that were sorely lacking in her life. And because he was, quite simply, the most magnificent-looking gentleman she'd ever seen.

It was pitiful, really.

And now she was allowing him to buy her gifts. Not only dresses and millinery, but stockings, chemises, and a new corset, too. Intimate gifts that touched her naked limbs. The kind of things a decent woman would never, ever accept from anyone save her wedded husband.

"St. Ashton always did keep his mistresses in high style," Felicity said. "He can't abide an unfashionable female. Everybody knows it."

Valentine tightened her hands in front of her. She reminded herself that Tristan had asked her to marry him. That the two of them had been discussing the future. *Their* future. She would not allow Felicity to plant seeds of doubt in her mind. Heaven knew there were enough there already. "My relationship with Lord St. Ashton is none of your business."

Felicity's dark eyes flashed. "*Relationship,*" she repeated, covering the word with scorn. "Is that what you call it? How pathetic you are. There is only one kind of relationship St. Ashton has with women like you. He—"

"He has proposed to me." Valentine heard the words before she realized that she'd said them. No doubt she looked as shocked as Felicity. They both seemed to have lost their color. And they were both standing stock-still, staring at each other with wide, startled eyes.

"You're a liar!" Felicity said.

Valentine attempted to affect an air of unconcern. She wasn't certain she succeeded. "Believe what you will."

Felicity took a step toward her. The enormous flounced skirts of her pink-and-white-striped afternoon dress brushed the edge of Valentine's own skirts, pressing them back against her legs. "You stupid little cow. If you think he cares for you, you're a bigger fool than ever I thought you were."

"I daresay I am." Valentine folded her arms at her waist to stop her trembling.

"If he's proposed to you, it's only because his father is here. The Earl of Lynden saw the two of you together in the conservatory, didn't he? There was nothing else for St. Ashton to do but make an honorable gesture." Felicity took another step forward. "Everything he's done for you is only for show. He doesn't mean any of it. St. Ashton never *means* anything. It's all sport to him."

Valentine's eyes were beginning to smart. "Is that all? Have you anything else to say to me?"

"Only this." Felicity was a breath away from her now. Close enough to strike her if she wished. Or to pull her hair if she wished. She did neither, choosing instead to do something—to promise something—far worse. "I'm going to tell everyone I know what a slut you are," she said, smiling. "No one in society will ever hire you again, not even as a scullery maid. The only work you'll be able to find in England is on your back."

Valentine lifted her chin. Her cheeks were burning and she could feel her pulse beating an erratic rhythm in her throat. "If you're quite finished," she said.

Felicity reached for the doorknob, opening the door with a hard jerk.

Valentine moved out of her way just in time. Had she lingered, she knew Felicity Brightwell wouldn't have scrupled to knock her down. As it was, Valentine could only stand there and watch the daughter of her former employer stride away down the hall, her enormous wire crinoline swinging wildly with every angry step.

After a long moment, she shut the door and latched it. And then she sank down on the edge of her narrow bed. The mattress sagged beneath her and the heap of white, ribbon-tied boxes tilted and fell. Several packages slid to the floor at her feet. She took a deep breath, and then another. By the time she regained her composure, any lingering happiness from her journey with Tristan—any pleasure at her beautiful new things—was gone. It had all turned to ashes in her mouth. Burned away by Felicity's words and by her own resurgent sense of right and wrong.

She looked numbly around the cramped bedroom. Only yesterday morning she'd been copying a psalm into her mother's book of Bible verses and longing for the day when she could join a mission in India or China. Goodness sake, she'd been contemplating learning Hindustani! And then, less than twelve hours later, she was in the arms of man. A veritable stranger. Clinging to him and kissing him.

What in heaven was wrong with her?

Chapter Nine

Sometime later Valentine descended from her room. The house was bustling with preparations for dinner, servants trotting up and down the threadbare halls in answer to the summons of their masters and mistresses. She walked briskly past them, her head down. She was so intent on avoiding any curious stares or impudent remarks that she didn't see Mrs. Ravenscroft emerging from her room near the second floor landing.

"Oh!" Mrs. Ravenscroft's much larger form collided with Valentine, nearly knocking her off of her feet. "Do be careful!"

Valentine staggered back a step before swiftly regaining her balance. "I beg your pardon!"

Mrs. Ravenscroft was only partially dressed, her embroidered silk dressing gown worn open over her corset and petticoats. "Where are you off to in such a rush?" she asked. "Dinner's not for another hour."

"Nowhere," Valentine said. "I'm only... That is...I—"

"If you're looking for Lord St. Ashton, you'll find him in the billiards room."

Valentine's cheeks flushed pink. "Oh, but I'm not—"

"And if you should see my maid along the way, do send her along to my room. She's supposed to be pressing my dinner dress but has been gone nearly half an hour." Mrs. Ravenscroft sighed. "What a disaster this house party has become. I'll be leaving in the morning on the eleven o'clock train to London. If you care to accompany me to the station, Miss March, you're quite welcome."

Valentine blinked in surprise. She didn't know what to say. Mrs. Ravenscroft's offer was kind. Unexpectedly so. But there was nothing for her in London—no friends, no family, and certainly no prospect of employment. Her only alternative to marrying Tristan was a third-class ticket back to Mrs. Pilcher in Hartwood Green who would, in turn, probably bundle her off to be companion to an elderly tyrant somewhere at the edge of the world. Or worse.

"I'm obliged to you, ma'am," she said at last. "But—"

"But you'll take your chances with St. Ashton." Mrs. Ravenscroft's red-rouged mouth tilted up in an indulgent smile. "I can't fault you. He's very handsome, isn't he? But I wouldn't depend on him, Miss March. St. Ashton has a well-earned reputation for being unreliable with the ladies. We none of us hold his interest for very long and I've seen many a broken heart that might have been avoided."

"My heart is not in danger," Valentine said quickly.

Mrs. Ravenscroft gave her a pitying look. "No, indeed. Forgive the advice. It was kindly meant." She inclined her head and then, after one last look down the hall for her errant maid, withdrew back into her bedchamber, shutting the door behind her.

Valentine was shaken by the exchange. She stood there a moment, staring blankly at the intricate inlaid pattern of the closed door.

And then she resumed her journey down the stairs.

She didn't know where the billiards room was and had to ask a passing footman for directions. He pointed her toward a room just beyond the Fairfords' library. It was down a dark, narrow hallway. Fairford House had not yet been fitted for gas, and the candles in the wall sconces stood unlit.

A faded Aubusson runner muffled her footfalls as she approached the door. She heard the sound of wooden balls clacking accompanied by the deep murmur of male voices.

"You can hardly cut off my allowance now," St. Ashton was saying in a bored, drawling voice. "Not now I'm engaged to be married." The balls clacked again. "What would people say?"

Valentine stopped in her tracks.

"You won't marry her," Lord Lynden replied. He sounded cross. And very, very tired. "If I doubted it last night, I know it today."

"You're very sure of yourself." There was another loud clack as a billiard ball was hit with force.

"I am," Lord Lynden said. "You would not have been so reckless with a lady you intended to marry. Driving her to York? Accompanying her to a dressmaker as if she were one of your doxies? By God. You're determined to ruin the gel."

"What would you have had me do?" Tristan asked. "Avoid her? Pretend last night never happened?"

"I would have had you here. Ready to leave at dawn as we agreed."

"Leave for where exactly?" Another billiard ball clacked—this time with all the ominous fury of a rifle shot.

Valentine nearly jumped out of her skin. It was enough to startle her out of her stillness. She was no eavesdropper. And she'd already heard quite enough. The exchange between Tristan and his father, coupled with the words of Felicity Brightwell and Mrs. Ravenscroft, made her sound like the most unwanted, pathetic creature in the world. But she refused to be made to feel that way. She'd behaved injudiciously—wantonly, even—but she wasn't pathetic.

She walked through the open door of the billiards room.

Tristan was in his shirtsleeves, his black cravat loose round his neck. He was leaning over the billiards table, in the midst of lining up his cue, when his gaze lifted toward the doorway. The expression in his eyes was hard to read, but she knew she must have startled him for, in the next instant, he fumbled his shot.

"Forgive me," she said. "I've distracted you."

Tristan straightened. "You have." He set aside his cue and walked around the table. "And I hope you'll stay awhile and distract me again. My father's company has grown tedious."

The Earl of Lynden rose from his chair and made her a bow. "We've been discussing marriage, Miss March. A damnable topic." He offered her his arm and, when she took it, led her past the billiards table toward a cluster of leather armchairs at the opposite end of the room. "We've also been discussing your good self. But perhaps you heard?"

She refused to pretend ignorance. "A very little."

"Would you care for a drink, Miss March?" Tristan asked. "A glass of sherry?"

"If you please." She seated herself in the chair nearest the fireplace. The flames had dwindled to embers, and a faint cloud of smoke drifted out into the room. It had likely been an age since the chimneys were properly swept.

Lord Lynden took a seat across from her. Beside his chair was a marble-topped table on which sat three crystal decanters filled with spirits. Tristan unstopped one of them and poured her out a small glass of pale amber liquid.

"Here you are," he said.

She took the proffered glass, giving the contents a dubious look. She knew what sherry was. Of course she did. But she'd never actually tasted it. Papa hadn't kept anything stronger than seasonal cordial at the vicarage and, since her time in Lady Brightwell's employ, she'd subsisted mainly on weak cups of tea.

Today, however, she'd already tasted ale. A shocking thing, in and of itself. Well, in for a penny, in for a pound. She raised the glass to her lips and took a healthy swallow.

And instantly grimaced at the bitter, burning taste of alcohol in her mouth.

"Don't tell me the Fairfords' sherry has gone off," Tristan said.

"I beg your pardon?" Valentine choked.

He was watching her with keen interest. "Your face is screwed up as if you've just sucked on a lemon. Is it the sherry?"

She fixed him with a reproving glare. His own face remained utterly inscrutable. Except for his eyes. They were quite plainly laughing at her.

"I can pour you a glass of something else if you like," he said. "The brandy here is first-rate, I can attest."

Oh, the wretched man!

She made an effort to compose her features when what she really felt like doing was running back upstairs and rinsing her mouth out over the washbasin. "No, thank you, my lord," she said, setting aside her glass.

"Never liked sherry myself," Lord Lynden remarked. "Awful stuff."

"It's a lady's drink," Tristan said dismissively. He didn't sit down with them, merely stood against the mantelpiece, his arms folded in front of him. It wasn't a very welcoming posture. "You're not dressed for dinner, Miss March. I take it you don't plan to join Lord and Lady Fairford at table."

"Indeed not," she said. "And you, my lords?" She looked between Tristan and Lord Lynden. "Will you be dining with the other guests this evening?"

"Not I," Lord Lynden said. "I'll be ordering a tray in my room."

"A decision the whole party will undoubtedly thank you for," Tristan said.

"While your presence, I'm sure, would be sorely missed," Valentine retorted.

"By one or two ladies at least," he replied without batting an eye. "Regrettably, I'll have to disappoint them. I intend to drink my dinner."

Lord Lynden frowned his disapproval. "With that," he said, moving to rise from his chair, "I will bid you both goodnight."

"My lord," she said. "If you could spare a moment longer. I'd hoped to discuss… That is… I came to tell you that I have come to a decision about my future."

Tristan looked at her with sudden alertness.

"Have you now?" Lord Lynden asked.

"Yes, sir. It's something Lord St. Ashton said that gave me the idea. Something about their being a great many Caddington relations who might wish to know me."

"There might well be," Lord Lynden said. "I've been thinking of one or two likely Caddington ladies myself. Not as high sticklers as the rest of the lot. A bit more open-minded."

"Are there such ladies?" she asked.

"One in particular comes to mind. Lady Hermione Caddington. A distant spinster cousin of your mother."

"Hermione Caddington?" Tristan sounded vaguely horrified. "The one who used to wear that outrageous Bloomer costume?"

"Reform dress," Lord Lynden mused. "Yes, yes. She was a bit of an original in her day."

"That's one way of putting it," Tristan said dryly.

"And you think she might be willing to meet me?" Valentine couldn't conceal the hope in her voice.

"We shall soon see. I sent her a wire this morning."

"*What?*" Tristan's face darkened with irritation "Without consulting me?"

Lord Lynden glared at his son. "And how was I to consult with you while you were gallivanting around York for the better part of the day?" he demanded. "No. I consulted my own judgment, sir. The more options Miss March has, the better."

Valentine leaned forward in her chair, hands clasped tightly in her lap. "What do you suggest, my lord?"

"St. Ashton informs me that you're opposed to staying with my son and daughter-in-law in Devonshire over the next year while he gets his property in order."

"Not opposed, but…I confess, it's not my first choice. I wouldn't like to be among strangers for such an extended period of time. Not unless I've been employed by them for an honest wage."

"You'd rather work?"

"I'd rather not be a burden. To stay with anyone on sufferance…" She shook her head. "No, my lord. I wouldn't find it at all comfortable. And I can't think your son and his wife would enjoy it very much either."

Lord Lynden considered her from beneath furrowed brows. "Perhaps you might prefer travelling to London to see Lady Hermione? She's not a stranger. She's your family. And, unless I've greatly misjudged her character, it wouldn't take much convincing to persuade her to stand chaperone for you."

Tristan straightened from where he leaned on the mantelpiece. "What in blazes is this?" His deep voice was taut with sudden anger. "A bloody conspiracy? Am I to have no say at all in my own future?"

"It's not your future we're discussing," Lord Lynden said. "It's Miss March's future."

"The two are one in the same," Tristan said. "Whether you like it or not, Miss March and I are going to be married."

Valentine could feel the tension between Lord Lynden and his son vibrating in the smoky air of the billiards room. The atmosphere fairly crackled with it. She looked between the two men. She didn't believe they hated each other. But there was a great deal of bitterness and disappointment on both sides. And she was certain it didn't help that, at present, Lord Lynden held the purse strings.

"I think I should like to go to London," she said.

Tristan looked at her. "Valentine—"

"I don't want to stay here any longer," she said. "After what happened last night…"

"Quite so," Lord Lynden agreed.

"It's become intolerable," she said. "I want to leave as soon as possible."

Lord Lynden nodded. "And so we shall. At dawn. As we should have done today." He rose. "I must speak to my valet. And I must write to Lady Hermione. If you'll excuse me, Miss March, I shall bid you good night."

"Good night, my lord. And thank you."

Lord Lynden acknowledged her thanks with an inclination of his head before levelling a quelling glance at his son. "St. Ashton. Pray don't drink yourself into a stupor this evening."

Valentine watched the Earl of Lynden walk from the room. When he was gone, she turned to Tristan. "You're not really going to drink your dinner, are you?"

"Does it matter?"

"Of course it matters," she said. "In truth, I wish you wouldn't drink at all."

"Don't judge all drink by your unfortunate experience with the Fairfords' sherry. Some alcohol is really quite good. Effective, too. It helps a man to round the corners, as they say. To plane away the asperities of existence."

"I haven't the slightest idea what any of that means. It sounds like utter nonsense."

"It means, my little innocent, that at times strong drink does a damned good job of making life more bearable."

"Is life so unbearable for you, my lord?"

"*My lord*," he repeated. "We regress." He moved from the fireplace to take his father's abandoned chair. Once seated, he fixed her with a brooding stare. "If you wanted to go to London to find a willing Caddington relation, why didn't you come to me? Why approach my father?"

He looked like a great predatory cat sprawled in the leather armchair. All long, muscled limbs and coiled strength. But there was something else there, too. Some emotion intertwined amongst the magnificence of his physical presence. Was he disappointed in her? Was he…

Great goodness.

Was he *hurt*?

She moistened her lips with the tip of her tongue. "I did come to you. I didn't know your father would be here as well. How could I?"

"And now he's taking you off to London without so much as a by-your-leave." Tristan raked a hand through his hair. "You're slipping away from me. I can see it. I can feel it happening, but I don't know how in the devil I'm supposed to stop it."

"I'm not slipping away from anyone. I'm right here."

"You are now. And for a few moments today, I truly believed—" He broke off with a faint, wry smile. "Stupid of me, I know, but I thought I could make you happy. A great blow to my conceit, I'm sure."

The butterflies in Valentine's stomach stirred to life. "I enjoyed our time together today very much. Truly I did. But no one can make anyone else happy. Not really. We all of us are responsible for our own happiness. Our own contentment. We can't seek it in other people."

"Can't we?" His expression softened almost imperceptibly. "*You* make me happy."

Her heart performed a queer little somersault. "Do I?"

"Very much."

"But how? We hardly know each other."

"I've kissed you," he said. "I've held you fast in my arms."

She could feel the heat of her blush as it swept from the collar of her Garibaldi blouse, up the column of her throat, and into her face. It burned like wildfire. "Yes, but…it hasn't even been twenty-four hours since you…since our encounter in the conservatory. That's scarcely any time at all."

"Counting the minutes, are you?"

She frowned at him. "I wish you wouldn't tease me."

"I'm a brute and a bully. I thought we established that last night."

"And I thought you promised to change."

He shrugged.

Valentine could have happily throttled him. In a rustle of skirts, she stood from her chair. She could no longer pretend they were just two people, sitting together in front of a smoking fire, having a civilized discussion about an abstract future. Her nerves were too jangled. Her feelings too raw. She strode to the billiards table, arms folded across her midsection. She heard the leather of Tristan's chair creak as he rose to follow her.

He wasn't as uninterested in what she had to say as he pretended.

She turned to face him. His hair was rumpled, his untied cravat hanging low on one side and short on the other. He looked tired and more than a little defeated. "I've heard things about you, you know," she said.

He didn't appeared to be the least impressed by this revelation. "Oh?"

"Since we were discovered together in the conservatory last night, the entire household has been at great pains to inform me that you're unreliable. That everything in life has been a sport to you. That you don't mean the half of what you say."

"They're right," he said. "It's all true. Every word."

"I don't doubt it." She saw him wince, but soldiered on. "They've also told me you proposed to me merely because your father's here. Because you wanted to make a show of having done the right thing."

"And you believe that."

"Do you deny it?"

Tristan was silent for a long moment. "I don't know if I can," he said at last. "Not in all honesty."

Valentine's heart sank. "I see."

"I don't think you do. My father had just exiled me and cut off my funds. Earlier he'd intimated that if I married and set up my nursery he would reconsider his decision." His fingers speared through his disheveled hair once more. "It must have had some impact on my proposal, mustn't it? How could it not have? And yet…when I knelt before you and asked you to marry me, I swear to you, I wasn't thinking of my fortune. And I was certainly not thinking of my father."

She exhaled an unsteady breath. And then she nodded. "I believe you."

"But you believe everything else as well. All the damning truths about my character."

"I would be a fool not to."

"And you're no fool."

"No, I'm not, but…" Her words came out in a rush of feeling. "I've put my faith in you, sir. And I have precious little faith left to spare. Don't you dare let me down, Tristan. Don't you dare break my heart."

Tristan stared down at her, stunned. "Do I have your heart, Valentine?"

Her mouth trembled. "I'm very much afraid that you do. Against all better judgment."

He searched her face, his dark eyes lit with a fierce tenderness that made her pounding heart stutter. She thought he would embrace her. A stupid girlish fancy! But he made no move to take her in his arms. Instead, he lifted his hand to her face and set the back of his fingers, very gently, against the curve of her cheek.

It was the barest touch. A mere caress of his knuckles on her skin.

But he was close. So close that she could feel the masculine heat from his body. Could smell the seductive scent of his expensive shaving soap.

Her lashes briefly fluttered closed, her bosom rising and falling on a tremulous, indrawn breath.

"What a mad little creature you are," he said huskily. "Didn't anyone ever warn you about men like me?"

"Often," she said. "And often."

"It never occurred to you to listen?"

"I listened. My whole life I listened. Until yesterday…" Her words trailed off as Tristan bent his head and pressed his lips to her brow. They lingered there, warm and firm, for a long while.

And her heart stopped. It simply ceased beating. She had a vague, ridiculous notion that it had swooned into a faint. Indeed, she wasn't entirely sure how she remained standing. At the touch of his lips, her knees had gone as weak and wobbly as a blancmange.

She waited for his mouth to find hers as it had last night. She waited for him to take her lips in a searing, soul-scorching kiss. But he didn't kiss her. Perhaps he didn't wish to. Perhaps…

"Tristan," she murmured.

"Yes, sweet?"

"Have you had a great deal to drink this evening?"

He stilled. "Why do you ask?"

She felt his breath against her forehead. "Have you?"

"Not a great deal." He drew back to look at her. "Why?"

"Yesterday…when you kissed me…"

His dark brows lifted in surprise. "You think that was because I was drunk?"

"You said you were a trifle disguised."

"A few glasses of wine, nothing more. Liquid courage. It prompted me to follow you into the conservatory. But kissing you…" His expression warmed. "Valentine, I wanted to kiss you in the folly—when I was wet, irritable, and cold sober." He paused. "I want to kiss you now."

A flicker of anticipation awakened within her. It was followed swiftly by shyness and an all too familiar feeling of uncertainty. "Why don't you?"

He brushed his lips across her forehead again in a brief, whispering caress. "Because the door to the billiards room is standing open. Because I can hear the sounds of the other guests emerging from their rooms for dinner. Because, my darling girl"—she felt him smile—"last night I may have compromised you, but, contrary to my father's opinion, I have no wish to ruin you."

There was no swooning this time. Her heart beat hard and strong. And it swelled with affection for him.

She brought her hand to lay alongside his face. "Because you're going to do the honorable thing."

"Yes," he said. And then he turned his face into her hand and pressed a chaste kiss to her palm. "Because this time, for once in my benighted life, I'm going to do the honorable thing."

Chapter Ten

Despite all his best intentions, when the morning came, Tristan didn't return to London with Valentine and his father. He hadn't been permitted to do so. It would worsen the scandal, his father had said. And it would do nothing for Valentine's reputation to arrive in town on the arm of the city's most notorious libertine. Instead, his father had left Fairford House at dawn with Valentine in tow. They'd driven to the railway station to catch the fast train to London.

As for himself, he settled in the back of his travelling coach—his coachman driving the horses, not toward London, but toward Northumberland.

He hadn't told Valentine. There'd been no time. Hell, he hadn't even seen her this morning. They'd parted last night in the billiards room after an hour spent sitting and talking. There'd been no love words. No flirtation. He'd merely held her hand like a lad courting his first young lady, his thumb moving tenderly over her delicate knuckles as she confided in him about her visit from that spiteful witch Felicity Brightwell.

Even now, his jaw clenched to think of it.

And then that damned Celia Ravenscroft had gone and compounded the problem with her ominous-sounding warnings about his unsteady character.

Was it any wonder Valentine had decided so suddenly to seek out a sympathetic Caddington relation? Since her father's death, she'd had no one in the world of her own. No one on whom she could rely. During their trip to York he'd thought, foolishly, that she might come to rely on him, but his prim little vicar's daughter was too sensible for that. And he couldn't blame her. He'd given her precious little evidence that he possessed any steadiness of character.

And now she was going to London, the city which formed the primary backdrop for his more than a decade's worth of depravity.

Tristan stared, unseeing, out the window of the rumbling carriage. The passing landscape was a blur of gray skies and stark, frostbitten hills.

Well, she would learn soon enough that the Viscount St. Ashton hadn't once in his life proven himself capable of being faithful to a woman. There were dozens of ladies of Felicity Brightwell's ilk in London. Dozens of ladies he'd either spurned outright, debauched and deserted, or dallied with for a month or two before severing the relationship with a vague note and a parting gift of jewelry from Rundell and Bridge. Any one of those ladies would be more than willing to inform Valentine what a selfish, heartless bastard he was.

"Which is precisely why you must stay away from London," his father had said earlier that morning. "And away from Miss March."

Tristan had been standing with his back to his father. He was still in his dressing gown. His travelling cases lay open on the bed. They were half-packed for the journey to London. "For how long?" he'd asked.

"A few months. Possibly longer."

"In other words, you would have me stay away from Miss March for a year. Just as you originally planned."

"The Caddingtons will be loath to accept her as it is. If they learn of her association with you—"

"You need say no more, my lord," Tristan had said sharply. "I comprehend your meaning."

When his father had gone, he'd swept the cases from his bed in a crashing burst of anger. And then he'd sat down at the writing desk and dashed off a letter to Musgrove, directing him to board the next train to Northumberland.

If he was to be barred from returning to London, he might as well travel to Blackburn Priory and see what could be done with the place. And if he must go into exile, so too must his meddling secretary.

As for Valentine March…

His father had said he'd explain things to her. That it was better not to linger. Better not to enact a dramatic farewell scene. Tristan had reluctantly agreed. He'd instead taken his leave of Valentine in a hastily scrawled note. Not because he didn't wish to say goodbye to her in person, but because he couldn't bear to see the look of disappointment in her eyes when he did so.

He was a coward.

"I'll write to her again," he'd told his father as he handed him the note. "Often. I'll not have her think me inconstant."

The Earl of Lynden had shaken his head. "She can't receive letters from you while staying with one of the Caddingtons. Not you or any man. It would be gravely improper."

"Under other circumstances, perhaps. But Miss March and I are engaged to be married."

"Your betrothal has not yet been announced. Nor will it be. Not for six months at least."

Tristan had gone perfectly still.

"You've overwhelmed the gel in your usual fashion," his father had continued. "Now you must leave her be awhile."

"Or else," Tristan had replied. "That's the threat, isn't it? Do as you say in this matter or risk being cut off from all means of support."

"Damn you, boy, I would have thought you'd want to protect Miss March. To do everything in your power to shield her good name. I've seen the way you look at her. You have a tenderness for her. Or am I mistaken?"

He'd glowered at his father, inwardly cursing the old devil for being so damned perceptive. "You're not mistaken," he'd said.

"Because she's an innocent."

"That's not it."

"Then why?"

Tristan had tried to make his father understand something he still didn't entirely understand himself. "She's different from the others. Sweet and earnest. She believes in things. Has faith in things." He'd looked away from his father before adding, "She has faith in *me*."

"And you don't want to disappoint her."

"I won't."

The coach jolted over another rut in the road, rattling the interior of the carriage and Tristan's bones along with it. He folded his arms and leaned back in his seat, his tall, beaver hat tipped down low over his eyes. He did have a tenderness for Valentine March. And what his father had said this morning made a good deal of sense.

Not that that made his advice any more palatable.

Nevertheless, he would go to Northumberland—something he'd done exactly once in the eleven years since his father had given him Blackburn Priory. He would go to Northumberland and he would attempt to make a success of his property. He only wished that doing the honorable thing wasn't so bloody uncomfortable.

Valentine sat across from the Earl of Lynden in the first-class railway carriage. His lordship was thoroughly absorbed in his newspaper—and had been since they boarded the train. On her own lap, a leather-bound book lay open. It was an old but obviously well-loved edition of Elizabeth Barrett Browning's *Sonnets from the Portuguese*, lent to her by the earl to read during the journey. She'd got no further than the first sentence before her mind had begun to drift.

Tristan hadn't even bothered to say goodbye.

The realization had left her angry and heartbroken by turns. Was this what he'd meant when he promised to do the honorable thing? To send her away from him without a word? After last night, when he'd pressed his lips to her forehead and held her hand, she'd thought…

But that was the trouble, wasn't it? She'd *thought*. When, in fact, Tristan hadn't said anything about his feelings. She'd informed him that he had her heart. And in exchange he'd said…what? That she made him happy? It was a lovely sentiment, to be sure, but it was hardly a declaration of enduring affection.

Valentine sighed heavily as she stared down at her book. She felt oddly deflated. Here she was, sitting across from Tristan's father and wearing clothing Tristan had given her, but she'd never felt farther away from him. The ache in her heart told her that he'd abandoned her. While the knots in her stomach warned her that soon, for the first time in her life, she would be facing a Caddington relation. Someone who had known her mother. And she would be doing so without the support of the man who had promised to marry her.

The man she very much feared she was falling in love with.

"Is the poetry not to your liking?" Lord Lynden asked.

She looked up with a start. He was watching her from beneath furrowed brows, his newspaper folded on the seat beside him. "What? Oh, no, my lord. It's very diverting."

"You haven't turned the page for the past hour," he observed.

Her cheeks colored. "Haven't I?"

"I trust you're not fretting over meeting Lady Hermione."

She smoothed a nonexistent crease in her skirts. For the journey, she'd worn one of the new dresses Tristan had bought her in York. It had a tight woolen jacket bodice and matching woolen skirts, swelled out to a magnificent size over her petticoats and crinoline. Made in a rich shade of mink brown and trimmed sparingly with military-style frogging and braid, it was really more of an afternoon dress than a carriage gown. Still, Valentine thought it more than sufficed for the journey. With her hair rolled up in a hairnet and a new hat perched atop her head, she looked neat as a pin. There would be nothing to criticize in her appearance, at least. Nothing by which Lady Hermione Caddington could outwardly judge her.

"Yes," she confessed. "I am rather."

"There's no need." Lord Lynden lifted his newspaper again and straightened the rumpled pages with a shake of his hands. She waited for him to say something more, but he seemed to consider the conversation at an end.

She looked out the window for a while, worrying her bottom lip between her teeth, before turning her gaze back to Lord Lynden. He wasn't very like his son. He didn't laugh or tease or flash a wolfish grin. Nor did he exhibit Tristan's penchant for brooding. He was, in short, not a temperamental man. He was stern and steady. Some might say cold-blooded.

But he'd been inordinately kind to her. Granted, it might well be that he was only being kind in order to get her away from his son—as far and as fast as possible. Whatever Tristan believed about his father's motives, Lord Lynden surely recognized that she was ineligible. She was a woman of no birth and no breeding. A bastard. A notorious one at that. He must be appalled at the very suggestion that such a person could one day ascend to the title of Countess of Lynden.

"My lord," she began in a small, hesitant voice.

The earl cast her a distracted glance from over the top of his newspaper. "What's that, Miss March?"

"Did Lord St. Ashton indicate… That is to say…did he happen to mention when he might join us in London?"

"If he's indeed gone to Northumberland, it will take him several months to assess the state of things at Blackburn Priory and begin repairs. I don't expect we'll see him until after the New Year."

Valentine fidgeted with one of her gloves. His answer wasn't quite the one she'd been hoping for.

And what in heaven did he mean, if Tristan had indeed gone to Northumberland? Where else in the world would he have gone?

"Won't he come back for Christmas?" she asked.

"Can't say he shared many of his plans with me. It was early hours and he was in a black mood. St. Ashton doesn't normally rise before noon—not in my experience." Lord Lynden shook his newspaper again and resumed reading. And then he frowned. "Blast," he muttered. The newspaper was cast aside and he began to rummage through the interior pockets of his capacious travelling coat. In a moment, he withdrew a folded piece of notepaper. "Forgive me, Miss March. I should have given this to you at the station. In all that commotion with the porter, it entirely slipped my mind."

Valentine took the note from his extended hand. She didn't ask from whom it came. It was obvious to both her and her rapidly skipping pulse. She held the note in her lap until Lord Lynden returned to his newspaper. When he was well and truly occupied, she unfolded the sheet of paper and began to read.

My Dear Miss March,

I've been exiled to Northumberland for the next several months. I'm told I must give you time to look about you. Pray do so. But know this: while you're confronting a bevy of over-proud Caddingtons, I'll be embarking on a far more perilous mission. I'll be alone, serious and sober, laboring to restore Blackburn Priory and endeavoring to justify your faith in me. When we meet again in the months to come, I hope you'll find me a better and worthier man. Until then, I remain your flawed, but still very much devoted,

St. Ashton

Valentine's cheeks warmed as she read Tristan's message a second time. She might have read it a third time, but she sensed that Lord Lynden was once again observing her from over the top of his newspaper. She carefully folded the sheet of notepaper and slipped it into her reticule.

"I assume that all is now right with the world?" Lord Lynden said.

Her blush deepened at the earl's dry tone. "Yes, I feel much better now, thank you."

He regarded her with a thoughtful expression. "Take care, my dear. Many a lady has fancied she would be the making of my son and many a lady has been disappointed."

Valentine wished people would stop warning her about Tristan's unreliability. It was fast becoming exasperating. "Lord St. Ashton shall be the making of himself. I have nothing at all to do with it."

"No? Well, I commend you on your good sense. It's a commodity that's been in short supply of late." He paused. "I expect your father, the vicar, was a sensible fellow."

"He was, sir."

"Sensible enough to marry your mother."

She experienced a twinge of discomfort. Reticence about her mother was deeply ingrained. It felt wrong to go from never speaking about her to casually discussing her with strangers. "I fear that good sense had precious little to do with it. My mother was very beautiful. Or so I am told."

"You've been told correctly. Sara Caddington was one of the great beauties of her time."

"I never saw her. I wish I had, but there's not even a likeness to remember her by. She died so suddenly. They'd only been married a few months. And then I was born and…she was gone."

"If you would like to know what your mother looked like, you need only consult your glass. You resemble her to an extraordinary degree."

"You're very kind to say so, my lord. But I know very well that I'm not a great beauty." She added, quickly, "And I'm not fishing for a compliment, sir. I'm simply stating a fact."

"A fact of which St. Ashton must have disabused you within the first ten minutes of making your acquaintance."

"No, indeed. He's never remarked upon my appearance. That is…except to tell me how appalling he finds my clothing."

It wasn't completely true. He'd told her she looked becoming in her new dresses, hadn't he? And he'd told her that she blushed very prettily. It wasn't the same as calling her beautiful, but the memory of it pleased her nonetheless.

She settled back into her seat. They had been travelling for more than an hour. The sounds of the train had become so much background noise. The screech of metal. The hiss of steam. The deep vibration in the railway carriage as the wheels trundled over the track. "Was my mother truly betrothed to a duke?" she asked.

His lordship inclined his head in acknowledgment. "The Duke of Carlisle. He was an older man. Too old. They were poorly suited. Had her father chosen someone else for her—"

"Then I wouldn't have been born."

"Quite so. It's one of the many vagaries of fate. A coincidence here. A missed opportunity there. A handful of serendipitous encounters. Just as was your presence at that reprehensible house party."

"And yours, sir," she reminded him.

Lord Lynden scowled. "But for my son, I wouldn't have been there. St. Ashton shouldn't have been there either. It's been years since he last attended the Fairfords' annual Bacchanalia. For that's what those gatherings are, Miss March. I shan't beat about the bush. The entire place and everyone in it is a scandal. I can't think what prompted my son to return there."

"I believe he's unhappy, my lord."

He gave an unsympathetic snort. "Unhappy, is he? If so, he has no one to blame but himself."

"You take a hard view."

"I take a realistic view. St. Ashton has spent the better part of his life sowing wild oats. Is it any wonder he should wake up one morning to discover he's left with nothing but a fallow field? A depleted patch of barren soil? The problem is of his own making. And the remedy, as I see it, is a fairly plain one."

Her mouth tilted with reluctant amusement. "Crop rotation?"

"In a manner of speaking."

"A human being is not a plant, my lord."

"And a man is not an animal, Miss March. He has duties. Obligations. We all of us must shoulder our responsibilities. Those who fail to do so are little better than beasts."

Her gaze dropped briefly to her hands. She mustn't idealize Tristan. He was a scapegrace. A scoundrel. Still…

"I think it can't be easy to live up to the expectations of the Earl of Lynden," she said.

For some reason, this made his lordship chuckle. "Come now, my dear. That old excuse might pass muster if St. Ashton was a boy, but he's a man of more than thirty years. My expectations have had no bearing on his conduct for two decades at least. That I can promise you."

She half smiled. "I daresay you're right. It's only that my own father had a great deal of influence on my behavior. All the way up until his death. At times, I confess, it could be rather stifling." Her smile turned faintly wistful. "How well did you know my mother, sir?"

"Not well at all," he said.

"Oh, but I thought—"

"No, Miss March. It wasn't I who was acquainted with Lady Sara. It was my wife, Eleonore."

Valentine's brows lifted. "Lord St. Ashton's mother?"

"They were childhood friends. Lady Sara was much younger than her, of course. By seven or eight years, if I remember. But they had grown up together on neighboring estates. Raised practically as sisters. When Eleonore and I married, Lady Sara was one of our wedding party."

"But…I don't understand. If my mother was like a younger sister to the Countess of Lyndon, then why—"

"Why didn't we help her?" Lord Lynden's face betrayed a brief grimace of self-disgust. "By that time, my wife had died. I wasn't myself for a long while. It's not much of an excuse, but there it is."

A sense of the injustice of it all settled in Valentine's chest. If only things had been different. If only someone had come to her mother's aid. "Is that why you're helping me, my lord?"

"The wrong done to your mother was no fault of mine," Lord Lynden said. "But when she found herself in trouble, I could have done more. Many in society could have done more. It's too late to make amends to Lady Sara herself, much to my regret. But I will try to do my best by her daughter.

It's what my wife would have wanted." He paused. "As for my son…"

"You don't believe he will honor his promise." Try as she might, she was unable to keep the tremor out of her voice. "You don't believe he'll come back for me or…or marry me."

"What I believe, Miss March," Lord Lynden said grimly, "is that you would be wise to put my son out of your mind for the next three months. And wiser still if you could manage to put him out of your mind altogether."

Chapter Eleven

London, England
Autumn, 1861

"Stand up, girl. Let me have a look at you."

Valentine rose from the tassel-trimmed sofa in Lady Hermione Caddington's opulent drawing room. She couldn't have envisioned a more intimidating setting for her first meeting with one of her mother's relations. The walls were papered in patterned yellow silk, the floors covered in rich Persian carpets. Plush settees and tufted ottomans vied for space with carved mahogany tables and button-back chairs and, from the ceiling, hung a truly magnificent crystal gasolier.

Taken altogether it made her feel the veriest country mouse.

She was still clad in her brown wool travelling gown. There'd been no time to change after arriving in London.

Lord Lynden hadn't even summoned his carriage from the station. Instead, he'd hailed a hansom cab and directed the jarvey to take them to Lady Hermione's residence in Belgrave Square—a stately townhouse where her ladyship lived alone, save for the presence of her servants and two overfed pug dogs.

An expressionless butler had conducted them to the drawing room in all decorum. But when Lady Hermione had entered moments later, she hadn't greeted Valentine as a guest. Nor had she acknowledged the presence of the Earl of Lynden. She'd merely strode in, her dogs trotting ahead of her like two medieval pages announcing the arrival of the queen, and lifted a pearl-encrusted lorgnette to her cool gray eyes.

Stand up, girl.

Every fiber of Valentine's being bristled with indignation, but she submitted to the arrogant inspection without a word. Her hands were clasped in front of her, her spine straight as a ramrod. She could feel the two pugs snorting around the hem of her voluminous skirts. One of the rude little beasts even poked its gargoyle-like face under the edge of her crinoline. She was sorely tempted to nudge it away with the toe of her boot.

"Primrose," Lady Hermione snapped. "Get out of there, you ridiculous creature."

Valentine cast a fleeting glance down at the offending pug as it withdrew from her skirts and loped off. The other pug followed.

Lord Lynden strolled up alongside her. "Well?"

After another long moment, Lady Hermione dropped her lorgnette. "It's exactly as you said."

"Naturally. If there were any doubt I wouldn't have wired you."

Lady Hermione gave an imperious wave in the direction of the sofa and chairs. "Sit, sit. We have much to discuss."

Valentine resumed her seat on the velvet sofa. Her stomach was trembling. She'd hoped that meeting one of her Caddington relations might be different. That it might make her feel as if she had a family of her own. A family who wanted her or, at least, wanted to know her better. But it didn't feel like that at the moment. Quite the opposite.

Lady Hermione seemed as if she were made of ice. At first, Valentine had thought it was only her appearance. She was a tall arctic blonde of middle years with sharp, chiseled features and a straight, uncompromising figure. Her eyes, though intelligent, lacked all warmth. And her clothing…

Valentine couldn't be entirely certain, but it seemed to her that Lady Hermione was wearing neither corset, nor crinoline. Her black silk gown fell about her frame in a wholly unstructured spill of fabric, a wide ribbon belt at her waist the only point of definition.

Such an ensemble might have softened another woman her age. Made her seem charmingly eccentric or even silly. On Lady Hermione Caddington, however, the clothing only served to make her look more formidable.

"I don't know how you find yourself involved in this, Lynden," she said.

"Does it matter?"

"It will soon enough. Everyone in London will want to know the story, down to the smallest detail. It will make the broadsheets, I'll wager. And when they see her…"

"Will they see her?" Lord Lynden asked quietly.

Lady Hermione's cold expression was almost militant. "If I have anything to say about it they will." At that, she summoned a footman and ordered tea. "We must make a plan," she said when the servant had departed.

"It will take some delicacy," Lord Lynden said.

Lady Hermione scoffed. "It will take boldness," she retorted. "And plain speaking." One of her pugs leapt onto the settee beside her. It circled round twice before curling up against an embroidered pillow. She rested a hand on its back. "You realize she will have to stay here?"

Lord Lynden inclined his head.

"And her association with you will have to end. Your own reputation is impeccable, my lord, but your son's reputation is another matter. We must take care that St. Ashton's name is not connected to this business. It would be ruinous at this stage and well you know it."

Valentine looked between the two of them. They were discussing her as if she were not even there. "I beg your pardon, ma'am," she began.

"Miss March," Lord Lynden warned.

She didn't heed him. "Lord St. Ashton is very much connected to this business. The two of us are engaged to be married."

Lady Hermione's gray eyes became positively glacial. They shot to Lord Lynden in accusation. "Is this true?"

He sighed. "Nothing has been formalized."

"In other words, this is another false promise of St. Ashton's. Made after a seduction, no doubt." She stood. "Well, my lord, this explains all."

Valentine opened her mouth to object, but Lord Lynden silenced her with a look.

"Now, Hermione—" he said.

"Don't dare patronize me, sir." She strode across the drawing room, her pugs trotting in her wake. Valentine feared she might storm out, never to be seen again, but Lady Hermione merely walked to an inlaid chest in the corner. She opened the topmost drawer and retrieved something from within. She stared down at it a moment.

"I have been accustomed to keeping this in my room," she said. "I brought it down this morning in anticipation of your arrival."

Valentine assumed she was speaking to Lord Lynden again, but when Lady Hermione returned to them, she didn't look at the earl. Instead, she sank down on the velvet-tufted sofa beside her. She smelled of lavender and herbal soap. It was a surprisingly reassuring fragrance.

"It was painted that last summer," she said. "Before the old marquess threw her to the wolves. I was away on the continent. By the time I returned to England, she was gone. Dead, they told me. Her and her child."

Valentine's gaze fell to Lady Hermione's outstretched hand. In the center of her palm she held a small framed portrait.

"Take it," Lady Hermione said. "It's yours now."

Valentine lifted the miniature from Lady's Hermione's hand with trembling fingers. It was a portrait of a young lady, painted in watercolor on ivory. A beautiful young lady with flaxen hair and wide, solemn gray eyes in a heart-shaped face.

"She was nineteen," Lady Hermione said matter-of-factly.

Valentine's throat tightened with emotion. "Oh," she whispered. She could think of nothing else to say. Her brain had transformed into porridge, her heart into a swollen lump in her chest. She swallowed back a swell of tears.

This, then, was the infamous Lady Sara Caddington. The shadowy, unknowable figure she'd dreamed of since she was first old enough to dream. Not a fallen woman or a wanton, but a girl. Just a girl.

"My mother," she said softly.

"Your mother," Lady Hermione concurred. "Now tell me—Miss March, is it?—exactly how big is this scandal of yours with St. Ashton? And when may we expect news of it to reach London?"

———◆·———

"Bloody blasted hell."

"Mind the mud puddle, my lord," Musgrove said.

Tristan shot his secretary a murderous glare. The puddle was, in fact, a several-foot-deep pit of thick black sludge, which now threatened to suck him under, feet first. He muttered another blistering oath as he attempted to extricate himself.

He'd already ruined one pair of boots during the course of this visit. He'd be damned if he ruined another.

"Why the devil is everything so wet?" he demanded. "It hasn't rained in four days."

"That would be the poor drainage in the north pasture, sir. I mentioned it in my report."

"Of course you did," Tristan said bitterly. They'd been at Blackburn Priory for two weeks and all Musgrove had done was write reports. Reports on the state of the crops. Reports on the state of the furnishings. Reports on the roof. Reports on the plumbing.

Tristan had no doubt that, in the past two years, Musgrove had sent just such reports about him to his father. Reports on how he'd parted from his last mistress and made no effort to obtain another. Reports on the days he'd spent drinking at home. Reports on how he'd fallen into a melancholy as black and bottomless as this cursed mud puddle appeared to be.

"One day, Musgrove," he said, "I shall quite happily write a report on how I gave you the sack."

"Yes, my lord," Musgrove said, unperturbed. He flipped open a page of the infernal little notebook he always carried with him. "As to the drainage…"

Tristan retrieved his handkerchief from the pocket of his greatcoat. "Go on."

"The former steward, Mr. Pope, recommended something be done last year. Trenches dug, tiled, and so forth. Alas, he was taken away with fever in the spring. I would have seen to the matter myself, but things had by that point reached—"

"Quite." Tristan gave his muddy boots another wholly inadequate swipe with his handkerchief. Higgins was going to strangle him. Two pairs of boots destroyed in two weeks. Not to mention the countless shirts, waistcoats, and trousers that had been soiled with mud, animal dung, and foul substances of every description.

"I'm treating stains from dawn 'til dusk," Higgins had complained only that morning. "I accept we are in the country now and a certain amount of filth is to be expected, but a valet can only take so much abuse, my lord."

At this rate, Tristan reflected, before the month was out, he would be obliged to order a new wardrobe from his tailor. Either that or hire a new valet. Good God, was there nothing about Blackburn Priory that came cheaply?

"You had better add drains to your list." He balled up his mud-splattered handkerchief and thrust it into the pocket of his greatcoat. "Better yet, add a new steward. You can hire him along with the rest of the servants on market day."

"A steward is not the sort of fellow one finds at a Mop Fair." Musgrove turned another page of his notebook. "However, I do have a recommendation from Lord Lynden. It seems his steward at Lyndwood Hall has a younger brother who's anxious to—"

"Brilliant. Another spy. By all means hire him."

"Yes, my lord. I'll send for him without delay."

Tristan resumed his thankless trudge through the pasture. The old water mill was just over the next rise, or so Musgrove had said. They might have ridden there, but he had no desire to see his riding horses subjected to the elements. One of them was already suffering from thrush and another had lost a shoe in the mud on the day of his arrival. They were town horses. Meant for Rotten Row, not rotten weather.

"What I need," he muttered, "is a pair of drays."

"Shall I add them to the list, my lord?"

Tristan supposed he could afford them. He still had what was left of his quarterly allowance. Not to mention those portions of his allowance he'd managed to save over the past two years. It was amazing how little coin a man expended once he grew tired of debauchery. Instead, that coin had sat in the bank, untouched, accumulating a tidy sum of interest.

But it couldn't last forever. And, though he might still be heir to one of the greatest fortunes in England, he'd be damned if he'd spend another year dependent on an allowance from his father.

"No," he said. "There are to be no unnecessary expenses."

"As you say, my lord."

He stopped at the top of the rise and looked out across the wet rolling hills. Down another slope he could see the stone façade of the dilapidated water mill. Situated on a bend of the River Coquet, it had once been the primary source of wealth and prosperity for the thriving market town of Harbury Morton.

"It's a shame it's fallen into such disrepair," Musgrove remarked. "The monks at the Priory charged a pretty penny for its use in their day."

"Their day being the year 1379."

"Somewhere thereabouts. If you'd like an exact date, my lord, I could consult—"

"It's no longer the fourteenth century, Musgrove. It's the nineteenth. And, lest you forget, Blackburn Priory is no longer a monastery." Tristan set off down the slope of the hill, his boots squelching in the mud. "Though, considering the circumstances," he said under his breath, "you may be forgiven for thinking so."

It was certainly not for lack of opportunity. Within his first two days in residence, the local squire had come calling with his unmarried daughter in tow. The next day, a neighboring widow had contrived to cross his path when he was driving into town. And then there was the matter of the hastily planned assembly ball to which St. Ashton had not only been invited, but urged to attend by the vicar, the village doctor, and no less than five meddling mamas who had had the temerity to appear on the doorstep of the Priory with baskets of cakes, biscuits, and preserves.

He hadn't attended the assembly. Nor had he succumbed to the advances of willing widows or marriage-minded squire's daughters. He'd gone to sleep alone each night in a cold bed, exhausted from the day's exertions.

His father had written at the end of the first week and informed him that Valentine was settled at Lady Hermione Caddington's townhouse in London. She was learning about her family, the letter had said. She was becoming better acquainted with her cousin. She was safe and comfortable and showing signs of growing contentment.

It was all so much nonsense.

As if he couldn't comprehend the real purpose of his father's letter. The old devil's true message was implicit in every line: Stay Away. Leave her be. Give her a chance to know her family. To find her footing. Give her a chance to meet someone better.

It was intolerable.

Tristan wasn't accustomed to waiting for the things he wanted. In the past, he'd always succumbed to his impulses, exercised his masculine urges, and then moved on. Delayed gratification could be diverting on occasion, but this…

This wasn't a game played with a mistress. It wasn't flirtation. This was painfully real. And, even as he trudged through his days at Blackburn Priory, reviewing ledgers, talking to neighboring farmers, and planning repairs, he was aware that somewhere, three hundred miles away in London, Valentine March was gradually slipping from his grasp.

"There's a steam mill in Morpeth," Musgrove said as they approached the water mill.

"Not an easy distance," Tristan observed.

"No, my lord."

"Why doesn't anyone build one here?"

"Lack of capital, I assume. And with there being no direct railway access to Harbury Morton, the town's not ideal for industry. It could never compete with Morpeth or Hexham, for example."

Tristan's gaze took in the sprawling stone edifice of the water mill. It had a damaged vertical wheel that now stood, unmoving. "I don't see why not." he said. "It may do quite well, on a small scale, if everything else weren't falling to pieces."

"Perhaps if someone of consequence were to take charge of the matter," Musgrove allowed. "Alas, everyone with ambition seems to have left the district. For greener pastures, as it were."

Tristan glanced at his secretary with narrowed eyes. He knew when he was being managed. Even so, it did nothing to dim the spark of interest that had lit within him at the sight of the mill. After two weeks of cold drudgery, a distraction was welcome. And if that distraction could, by any slim chance, lead to his being independent from his father, all the better. "Not everyone, Musgrove."

Chapter Twelve

For the next three weeks, Valentine lived in Lady Hermione's townhouse as a veritable prisoner. She was given a comfortable set of rooms. She had access to a well-stocked library. And she ate the finest meals on the finest porcelain plates, seated across from Lady Hermione at a carved mahogany dining table that had been polished by the servants until it shown like mirrored glass.

"You're not ready," Lady Hermione said whenever Valentine broached the subject of venturing out of doors. "And I'm still debating with Penelope and Euphemia about how best to manage your introduction into society."

Valentine met Lady Penelope and Lady Euphemia during her first week in residence. They were two elderly spinster cousins of the late Marquess of Stokedale. Like Lady Hermione, they had flaxen hair and doe-like gray eyes—features Valentine discovered were shared by many a Caddington female. And, like Lady Hermione, they were considered to be rather eccentric in opinions, manners, and dress.

They stared at her, inspected her, and interrogated her in turns. They marveled at her resemblance to her mother. They wondered about the identity of her father. And they made plans.

Her Caddington relations were *always* making plans.

The trouble was, the three of them never agreed on anything. Lady Hermione wanted to put Valentine up at her clubs and introduce her to her radical friends. The ones who debated dress reform and equal rights for women.

"She'll need to learn to make her own way in the world," Lady Hermione said. "And what better allies in the battle for feminine independence?"

Lady Penelope thought it best to take Valentine on a discreet visit to see her uncle, the present Marquess of Stokedale, and—as she said—let the chips fall where they may.

"There's no point in delaying it," she declared. "If he accepts her, we may have done with the matter. And, if he rejects her, as he most certainly will, then we'll all know how to proceed."

Most alarming of all was the course of action suggested by Lady Euphemia. She envisioned a grand ball to introduce the long-lost daughter of Lady Sara Caddington to society.

"A Christmas ball," she said. "With all the family in attendance."

Initially, these sorts of dramatic ideas sent Valentine into an agony of emotion. However, by the end of the second week, she began to take them in her stride. Not only that, she fell into some semblance of a household routine. A lonely routine, but a routine nonetheless.

Through it all, she never once heard from the Viscount St. Ashton.

Which wasn't a surprise, all things considered. She didn't believe he'd forgotten her. Indeed, she still had a great deal of faith in him. Never mind that that faith was chipped away at each day by her well-meaning relations.

Lord Lynden, as well, seemed to have disappeared into the ether. As the days passed with no word from him, she began to suspect that—having successfully deposited her with Lady Hermione—his lordship had washed his hands of her.

Sometimes, when she was alone and idle, she felt a creeping melancholy eating away at the edges of her existence. She fell prey to fears and doubts about her future. She suffered embarrassment and regret over her past behavior. And she worried herself silly about whether or not Tristan cared for her.

The rest of the time, however, the solitude wasn't so terribly difficult. In truth, it was quite welcome. She wrote to Mrs. Pilcher in Hartwood Green, informing her that she'd left Lady Brightwell's employ and was now staying with one of her late mother's relations in London. And she had plenty of opportunity to work on her book of Bible verses. She even began to try her hand at illustration, though, admittedly, she didn't have a fraction of her late mother's talent.

Her mother had begun the book while she awaited Valentine's birth, or so Papa had always said. She'd copied out the verses and illustrated them with sketches of flowers and foliage, stags and lions, and eagles and unicorns. Most of the illustrations had been done in ink or pencil and then filled in with watercolors. They were complemented by her mother's swirling script, quoting passages of her favorite Bible verses.

It had been an unfinished labor of love. A project that Valentine had hoped to one day complete herself. But now…

Felicity Brightwell had destroyed all but the one page. And even that was splotched with ink. The illustration was still visible, thank goodness. And Valentine knew the psalm her mother had quoted backwards and forwards. All that was left was to begin at the beginning. To attempt to reconstruct her mother's legacy to her from memory, one Bible verse and one rudimentary sketch at a time.

She was thus engaged on a Tuesday, during her third week in residence, when Lady Hermione entered the morning room with a newspaper in hand.

"The Brightwells have arrived in London," she said.

Valentine looked up from her work. She'd just finished copying out a verse she remembered as having been at the front of her mother's book. *Let the morning bring me word of your unfailing love, for I have put my trust in you.* It had been illustrated with a stag and a lion with an eagle flying overhead.

She put down her pen and flexed her hand. Her fingers were cramped and stained with ink. "Have they?"

"Just yesterday. It's here in the papers." Lady Hermione came to the desk and peered over her shoulder. "Is that a sketch of Primrose?" she asked. "No. It can't be. The proportions are wrong."

"It's meant to be a lion."

"With a corkscrew tail?"

"That's not the tail. It's part of the vine that grows around the illustration. See here? These are the flowers. And this is the tuft of grass beneath."

"Hmm. I daresay it will look more like a lion when you have painted it in."

Valentine doubted it. She wasn't an artist. Not by any measure. She rose from her chair to join Lady Hermione on the settee. A glance at the newspaper confirmed her distant cousin's report. Lady Brightwell and her daughter had returned to London for the Christmas season. They had taken up residence with friends in Park Lane.

"May we count on their discretion?" Lady Hermione asked.

Valentine shook her head. "Felicity as good as promised that she would tell everyone about what happened in Yorkshire. She's determined to ruin me."

Lady Hermione gave an unladylike snort. "Stuff and nonsense. How can she tell anyone anything without admitting to having been at the Fairfords' orgy herself?"

Valentine winced. She wished Lady Hermione would cease referring to that wretched house party as an orgy. She felt bad enough about having been there already. "Felicity never cares about the consequences of her behavior when she is in a temper. She'll say and do whatever she pleases. Whatever is most cruel."

"She sounds positively charming."

"Yes, well…she wanted to marry Lord St. Ashton quite desperately."

"Clearly. I expect she thought to lure him into an indiscretion at Fairford House and then trap him into marriage. A ridiculous plan. A man like St. Ashton can't be caught. A gentleman must have a sense of decency in order to do the right thing."

Valentine held her tongue. This wasn't the first time someone had alluded to Tristan's lack of honor—at least insofar as women were concerned—and she doubted it would be the last.

"How very tiresome." Lady Hermione sighed as she rose from the settee. "I had planned to wait until after the holiday, but if this Brightwell chit interferes..." She walked to the window and back again, brow creased in contemplation. "There is nothing for it," she said at length. "We shall have to pay a call on Stokedale."

Valentine's eyes widened in alarm. "Now?"

"No, not now. We'll go tomorrow morning. Stokedale mustn't hear about you from other quarters. It would be fatal to our cause." She cast a distracted look at the door. "It's early hours, but I must call on Penelope and Euphemia. They will wish to know all." She glanced back at Valentine. "I'll return by luncheon," she said as she moved to depart. "In the meanwhile, have Maisy prepare a solution for those ink stains on your fingers. A good soak should do the trick. We can't have you meeting your uncle looking like a renegade copy clerk."

When Lady Hermione had gone, Valentine returned to the little walnut desk in the corner and resumed her work. She was determined to finish her illustration before she subjected herself to one of the housekeeper's lemon juice soaks. But, upon lifting her pen, she realized that the news that tomorrow she would finally be coming face to face with the Marquess of Stokedale made any further drawing impossible. Her hands were too unsteady.

Andrew Albert Caddington, Marquess of Stokedale was her mother's only living sibling. He was a widower of one and fifty. The father of three boys and three girls, all of whom had now reached adulthood. He was a proud man, as the late marquess had been before him, and, according to Lady Hermione, set great store in the excellence of the Caddington bloodline.

When his younger sister, Lady Sara, had found herself with child, he'd taken his father's side in the matter, refusing to lift a finger when Lady Sara was cast out into the streets.

Valentine had never felt hatred for anyone. Everything within her rebelled against such an emotion. It was wicked and unchristian. But when she thought of the Marquess of Stokedale, something roiled inside her that must be very much akin to hatred.

The man had stood by and done nothing when his only sister had—as Lady Hermione so often put it—been thrown to the wolves. He'd done nothing when Valentine had written to him for help. It seemed that, as far as he was concerned, Lady Sara's memory and her bloodline could die out. Could be eradicated root and branch. He simply didn't care. She was a bastard, after all. A March, not a Caddington.

"And happy to be so," she muttered to herself as she set down her pen.

Papa hadn't been perfect. He'd been judgmental, often hypocritical, and always impossible to please. Indeed, the more she worked on the book of the verses, the more Valentine grew to believe that it was a task her father had set for her mother. A sort of penance for her sins, as it were. He'd always said she was guilty of wantonness. And yet…

When he'd found Lady Sara, nearly six months gone with child, weeping in the vestibule of his church, he had, ultimately, done the right thing.

Perhaps it was merely charity. Or merely infatuation. Whatever his reasons, he hadn't turned her away. He would never have let her and her unborn child starve in the streets. And he would never have allowed Valentine to be born without a name.

She looked down at her latest attempt at recreating her mother's book of verses with a critical eye. The lion did look a little like a pug dog, but the script was rather pretty. She'd managed to copy her mother's writing exactly, down to the last loop and swirl.

Let the morning bring me word of your unfailing love, for I have put my trust in you.

Now, if only she could remember the verses and illustrations for all the rest of the pages that Felicity had destroyed.

"Ma'am?"

Valentine turned in her seat at the sound of the butler's voice. He stood at the door to the morning room, his face as expressionless as it had been on the day of her arrival. "Yes, Ledsen? What is it?"

"You have a caller. A young gentleman. Most insistent. I've put him in the drawing room."

Valentine's pulse leapt into her throat. *Tristan*. He'd finally come for her. She stood. "Oh! Thank you, Ledsen!"

"Ma'am—" he began as she rushed past him out the door, "her ladyship wouldn't approve—"

"It's perfectly all right." Valentine lifted her skirts as she darted down the hall. The drawing room was on the second floor. After ascending the stairs, she slowed her stride and gave herself a chance to catch her breath. She mustn't appear overeager, despite the fact she'd been longing to see him for more than three weeks straight. She must appear calm and composed. Indifferent, even.

She smoothed her hands over her woolen day dress. And then she opened the door and entered.

A slender man of medium height was standing by the bank of windows, hat and gloves in hand. The morning sunlight turned his fair hair to gold. "Val," he said, smiling.

Her mouth fell open in horror. "*Phil?*"

———————◆———————

At precisely eleven o'clock on Tuesday morning, Tristan arrived at Lady Hermione's residence in Belgrave Square in a hired hansom. He'd taken the train down from Northumberland the previous day. A bloody miserable journey. But it had been worth it. He'd spoken to Lords Wroxham and Clithering, two of his old comrades in debauchery. They were always up for a gamble, whether it be gaming, racing, or women. Earlier that morning, ensconced in a private, smoke-filled room at his club, he'd attempted to persuade them to apply their adventurous spirits to the realm of business. Or, more precisely, to apply their money.

The meeting had been more successful than he ever could have hoped. He suspected this was owing, in part, to the fact that he'd approached both men after a night of heavy drinking and ribaldry. Indeed, he didn't believe either had even been to bed yet. Why else would they be awake at half nine in the morning?

Frankly, it was a miracle he was awake himself. But he'd become accustomed to rising early at Blackburn Priory. It wasn't only that a blasted cock crowed outside his window every morning at dawn, but that, with so many things to see to on the estate, it was necessary to make the most of the daylight hours.

Now back in London, he knew that morning calls didn't really take place until afternoon. But after all he'd gone through during the past weeks, he had to speak with Valentine. It would all be worth it if he could see her. If he could hear just one of her prim little sermons. It had been nearly a month since they had parted in Yorkshire. And he'd been pining for her like a dratted schoolboy ever since. It was ridiculous. Pathetic.

It was utterly intolerable.

He'd thought that, with time and distance, his attraction to her would fade. His father had believed it would. It was the sole reason he'd insisted on a long engagement. But, instead of fading, Tristan's feelings for her seemed to have grown stronger. To have solidified into something lasting and real.

Of course, there was every chance that, in her absence, he'd idealized her. Set her on a pedestal. And there was an equal chance that, in his absence, she'd come to her senses. That she'd realized that he wasn't a man worthy of her affections. That she'd discovered she no longer cared for him.

Tristan didn't like to think of that possibility. It made his heart ache in a completely unacceptable manner.

His heart.

And that was the hell of it.

He disembarked from the hansom cab and, after flipping a few coins to the jarvey, he bounded up the front steps of Lady Hermione's townhouse. A nervous excitement quickened his pulse. Perhaps he should have sent word that he was coming? Something to tell her when she might expect him? For all he knew, she might not even be at home.

But it was too late for second-guessing. He raised his hand and gave an impatient rap on the door with the brass knocker. The door was opened almost immediately by an elderly man in a dusty black suit. Lady Hermione's butler, presumably.

"Yes, sir?"

Tristan didn't wait for an invitation. He strode past the butler into the marble-tiled entryway. "Tell Miss March that St. Ashton is here to see her," he said as he divested himself of his hat and gloves

"Yes, my lord." The butler took his things and ushered him toward a modest room off the hall. "If you would be so kind as to wait in the morning room? Miss March is…" He trailed off, his eyes darting toward the second floor landing.

"Really, Val." A man's voice floated down the stairs. "That's not the way I remember it at all."

Tristan's followed the butler's gaze to the staircase in time to see a pale, fair-haired fellow descending. He had the face and figure of a romantic poet. The sort of anemic, prosing individual that village girls enjoyed swooning over. And beside him, clad in a handsome blue day dress, was Valentine.

His Valentine.

"Then your memory of the events in September is as addled as all the rest of you," she said. "We are *not* going to marry. We never were."

"Come now, my dear," he said. "Engagements are not so easily broken. One must honor one's promises."

Tristan's body tensed with outrage. He stepped forward. "On that I quite agree."

Valentine's gaze jerked to his with a start. Her lips parted on an indrawn breath. "Tristan."

"Miss March," he said, bowing. "Do introduce me to your friend."

Two spots of color appeared high on her cheeks, tinting her porcelain skin to rose. "My lord, may I present Mr. Phillip Edgecombe. Mr. Edgecombe, this is the Viscount St. Ashton."

"Miss March's fiancé," Tristan added. "Or hasn't she told you?"

Edgecombe descended the final step. Tristan was pleased to see that he was taller than the little parasite by over a head and outweighed him by at least two stone. "I fear that's not possible, my lord. You see, Miss March is promised to me."

"Is that so?"

"Yes, indeed. We grew up together in Hartwood Green. We have had an understanding of long duration."

Tristan lifted his brows. "What do you say to this, Miss March?"

Valentine's eyes went to the butler. He was standing near the door, looking damnably uncomfortable. She made a soft sound of exasperation. "If we must discuss this, let's not do so in the hall, gentlemen. Come into the morning room, both of you."

Tristan didn't budge. "Ah, but Mr. Edgecombe was leaving, wasn't he? I have no wish to detain him."

"I'm happy to explain the circumstances of my engagement to Miss March," Edgecombe said. "In the morning room or anywhere."

Valentine's expression tightened. "For the last time," she said, "there is no engagement. There never was one. When I left Hartwood Green, you made it very plain—"

"A misunderstanding," Edgecombe interrupted. "Which I've repeatedly explained."

"There is no misunderstanding." She looked at Tristan. "I wrote to Mrs. Pilcher to reassure her that I was all right. I told her I was staying with Lady Hermione. She relayed the information to Mr. Edgecombe and, believing me to be in line for some of the Caddington fortune, he's travelled here today to insist that we marry!"

"Has he, indeed."

"Yes," Valentine said. "And he's insinuated that, if I don't marry him, he'll sue me for breach of promise and have my name dragged through the courts! Have you ever heard of anything so dastardly?"

Edgecombe held up a hand in protest. "Now, Val. You know that's not what I said."

"It's what you meant!"

"But you must consider my sacrifice. A trip to London is not inexpensive. I came here relying on our agreement. When you say that you won't marry me, you're in breach of that agreement. It's a classic case, my dear. I consulted a solicitor on the subject and—"

Tristan drew himself up to his full height. "Did you, by God."

"Well, I must say that I did. For I had an inkling that Val would be difficult on the subject now that she is more comfortably off. And had I known she was in danger of losing her head to a man who is known far and wide as a—"

"Oh, don't say it, Phil," Valentine warned under her breath.

"By all means do, *Phil*," Tristan urged.

"I won't disparage you, my lord. I didn't come to town to make enemies. I came to settle things with Val and, once I have done, I shall return to Hartwood Green."

"Are things settled, Miss March?" Tristan asked her.

"To my mind."

"That's good enough for me," Tristan said. And with that, he grabbed hold of Phillip Edgecombe by his knotted cravat, hauled him up nearly off of his feet, and—forcibly—escorted him out the door.

Chapter Thireen

Valentine stood on the front steps of Lady Hermione's townhouse and watched, mouth agape, as Tristan tossed Phillip Edgecombe into the street. Phil staggered wildly, his arms circling like a windmill, but he didn't fall. She felt a surge of relief. As odious as he'd been to her, she didn't wish to see him seriously injured.

She caught Tristan's arm. "Pray don't hurt him."

Tristan turned on her. A lock of raven black hair had fallen across his brow. It did nothing to soften the ferocity of his expression. "If you care for him, tell me now, madam. You needn't mince words."

"Don't be stupid." She tugged his arm. "Come inside. Lady Hermione will never forgive me if we make a spectacle of ourselves in the street."

He allowed her to pull him back into the house. Ledsen shut the door behind them. Valentine couldn't bring herself to meet the old butler's eyes. In situations such as these, men almost always blamed the woman. And, in this instance, she supposed that it was her fault to some degree.

"I shouldn't have said anything to either of you in the hall," she said as she led Tristan into the morning room.

"Why the devil not?"

"Because Phil—I mean, Mr. Edgecombe—was being impossible. And I should have known that you would—"

"Behave true to character?"

"What?"

"A bully and a brute. You said that in Yorkshire once. Or something to that effect."

She stopped in the center of the morning room and stared up at him. A glowing warmth suffused her chest. It had only been a few weeks, yet he was even more handsome than she remembered. And infinitely more dear. "Yes, I suppose I did."

"Well, there you are."

Her gaze drifted over his face. Smitten, that's what she was. It was embarrassing really. Especially as the feeling was so obviously not mutual. Tristan returned her gaze with aristocratic indifference, or so it seemed to her. He appeared to be wholly unaffected by their reunion. While she was, by his very presence, transformed into a mass of melting treacle. "No one has ever stood up for me before," she blurted out. "Not in my entire life."

He gave her an arrested look. "Haven't they?"

"Never. And what you did just now… It was simply magnificent."

"It was brute strength. There's nothing particularly—"

"*You* were magnificent."

Tristan's lips tilted in a fleeting smile. He appeared faintly amused. Mildly diverted. He also appeared to be turning a dull red about the collar.

Valentine's eyes fell to his cravat. Good lord above! Had she just made the most notorious libertine in England blush like a schoolboy?

"You're very easy to impress, Miss March," he said.

She smiled up at him. "Why are you here? What are you doing in London? I didn't think I would see you again until the New Year."

"I came to meet with some gentlemen at my club. I had a rather pressing business proposition to discuss with them."

Her smile dimmed a little. What had she expected? A passionate declaration of love? Of course he hadn't come back for her. It was remarkably foolish of her to even entertain such thoughts.

She gestured to the silk damask settee. "Won't you sit down?"

"I'm too restless. But you sit, please."

She did, spending some little time arranging her skirts. She wished she'd worn a prettier dress. Something with a flounce or a few ribbons. Not that he seemed to notice what she was wearing. "What sort of business proposition? Is it something to do with Blackburn Priory?"

"In a manner of speaking." He rubbed a hand along the side of his jaw. "These last weeks I've been making an inventory of the Priory, as well as beginning some of the less costly repairs. Replacing rotted roof tiles and digging drainage trenches and so forth." He paused, frowning. "Are you at all familiar with the market town of Harbury Morton?"

She shook her head.

Tristan began to pace the room. "It has no industry. No direct rail access. But the farmers and landowners thereabouts produce an annual yield that far exceeds…"

Valentine listened in silence as Tristan went on to talk of crops, steam mills, and transport. She didn't fully understand it but was mesmerized by the intensity with which he tackled the subject.

When they had first met in Yorkshire, she had been drawn to him because he was kind and handsome, and because he had seemed lost and a little sad. He had needed her, even if only in some small way. But now, he was fairly brimming with confidence. He was happy. She'd known he would be. He was too inherently good to have kept on down the wrong path. Instead, he'd summoned the strength to make a change. It was one of the reasons she loved him so.

And one of the reasons, she feared she would lose him.

After all, what need did he have of her now? None at all. They were bound together by nothing more than his promise to marry her.

"It was the water mill that gave me the idea," he said. "In centuries past, it made Harbury Morton a thriving concern. But now, every farmer and landowner in the district is obliged to transport their crops to towns with working mills. If there were a way for Harbury Morton to have a steam mill of its own. And direct rail access to transport its crops, coal, and lime…"

"Is there such a way?" she asked.

"I believe there is," he said. "I've spoken to an industrialist in Newcastle who's been keen to build a steam mill in Harbury Morton these many years. The gentlemen at the Blyth and Tyne Railway are equally keen. In both cases, all it wants is investment. I already own the land."

"Perhaps your father—"

"No," Tristan said. "My father has nothing to do with this. If anything, I expect that my ventures in Northumberland might eventually set me free of him."

Valentine folded her hands in her lap. She wasn't sure what to say, so she remained quiet as Tristan's pacing took him to the small walnut writing desk on which her book of verses sat open. He stopped there, casting an idle glance down at her work.

"It's all rather ironic," he said.

"How do you mean?"

"I've come to believe that that's the very reason my father gave me Blackburn Priory. So that I might gain independence from him. He must have known the place was rich with possibility. Had I gone there years ago—had I taken the time—I might have seen it for myself."

"Everything happens in its season," she said. "That's what my father used to say."

"Very wise of him." He set his hand on the edge of the desk. "If only that season would have come sooner. Then I would have known…"

"Known what?"

"That my father never wished to see me fail. Quite the opposite. He hoped to see me succeed."

"Of course he did. Your father loves you very much."

He gave a short laugh. "Let's not get carried away."

"But he does," she insisted.

"I can't imagine why," he said. "I've been the greatest trial of his life. Had there not been intervening circumstances, I have no doubt he would have cut off my funds and cast me off into the proverbial wilderness."

The words she'd overheard outside the billiards room at Fairford House echoed in Valentine's mind. "By intervening circumstances, you mean your engagement to me."

Tristan didn't deny it. "My father wouldn't allow my future wife and children to live in penury. No matter how much I had disappointed him. A hard fact, but—" He broke off. "What is this?"

"I beg your pardon?"

His attention was fixed on the opening page of her book of verses. "This drawing."

She flushed. "It's meant to be a lion." She rose from her seat and went to his side. Her skirts brushed up against his leg. "I know it looks like a pug dog, but once I have applied the watercolors it should look a bit closer to my mother's illustration."

"What illustration?"

"From the front of the original book of verses. It was one of the pages that Felicity Brightwell destroyed. I can't recreate all of them, but I'm trying to draw some from memory."

"A stag facing a lion, each on their hind legs," he said thoughtfully. "And this I suppose is an eagle."

"With a crown of roses in his beak." She gave him a rueful smile. "My mother painted many variations of the design, but this was the most common. I always thought it a rather odd configuration."

Tristan looked up from the book. His eyes found hers. "Was your mother very religious?" he asked abruptly.

"No more than reason."

"Yet she named you after a saint."

She shrugged a shoulder. "Papa said she was trying to atone. To make things right with God before I was born. She can't have felt easy about having a child out of wedlock. And certainly not so far from home."

"Why did she choose Surrey, I wonder. What brought her there?"

"To our village?" Valentine frowned. She'd often wondered the same thing herself. "I suppose she must have simply run out of money. Before Papa found her weeping in the church, at Hartford Green she'd been staying for several days at an inn outside the village. She could no longer afford it."

Tristan looked down again at the book of verses. "The famous Caddington pride," he muttered.

"You think it was pride that brought her to Hartwood Green?"

"No," he said. "But I think—indeed, I would wager my last groat—that it was pride that kept her from returning home to Caddington Park."

Her brow furrowed in confusion. "I don't understand—"

"St. Ashton." Lady Hermione's voice rang out from the doorway. "How good of you to call on us."

Valentine turned from the desk with a start to see her distant cousin entering the drawing room. A rush of heat crept into her face at being caught alone with Tristan, and in such close proximity, too. She immediately moved away from him. "You're back early, ma'am."

"As you see."

"Were Lady Penelope and Lady Euphemia not at home?"

"They were, but there was no need to dally." Lady Hermione looked at Tristan. "To what do we owe the honor of this visit, my lord?"

Tristan greeted Lady Hermione with cool civility. "I'm in London on business. As I've been explaining to Miss March."

"Lord St. Ashton is seeking investors for a business venture," Valentine said. "A steam mill and a railway station in Northumberland."

"How enterprising of him."

"It's bound to be a great success."

"Indeed."

"And it will make him quite independent of Lord Lynden."

Lady Hermione's gray gaze slid to Tristan's face. "If that's so, then there will be no more need to marry in order to secure your income."

Tristan acknowledged this fact with a subtle inclination of his head. "No need at all, ma'am."

"And this is what you have come to tell my young cousin, I presume."

Valentine heartbeat quickened. She looked at Tristan, her eyes questioning. He wasn't calling off their engagement, was he? He couldn't be. Only a short time ago, he'd told Phil that the two of them were betrothed. If he didn't wish to marry her, then why…?

"I'm afraid that's a conversation for another day," Tristan said. His expression was unreadable, his voice reverting to the same tones of aristocratic indifference she'd heard him use in North Yorkshire. "I've already stayed too long. I've other appointments this afternoon."

"As do we," Lady Hermione said. "Tomorrow we'll be travelling to Caddington Park and we must make our arrangements."

Tristan's face betrayed the faintest flicker of surprise. "You're going to see Stokedale?"

"We are."

Valentine's stomach was trembling. She clasped her hands at her waist. When Tristan threw her a glance, she looked away. She couldn't bear it.

"You have no cause to do anything I ask, my lady," he said, "but I would beg you to notify my father. Allow him to accompany you."

"To lend us countenance?" Lady Hermione scoffed.

"To lend support to Miss March. I would go myself, but—"

"You most certainly won't!" Lady Hermione's bosom swelled with righteous indignation. "When I think of what I've had to endure. The lengths to which I must go to shield my cousin from gossip. That orgy in Yorkshire. Those odious Brightwell creatures. And now, Ledsen tells me, you've pitched a country gentleman into the street outside my own home! A country gentleman who's threatening lawsuits and scandal and having respectable people brought up on charges!"

"Oh no," Valentine said in horror. "He didn't, did he?"

Lady Hermione didn't answer. She was in too much of a passion. "No, St. Ashton. You shall not accompany us to Caddington Park. You've done quite enough for my cousin, thank you."

Tristan's face had gone hard as stone. "You need say no more, madam. You've made yourself abundantly clear."

"I trust I have." Lady Hermione strode to the door of the morning room and pulled it open. "Miss March? See our guest out, if you please."

Valentine did as she was bid, walking out the door and down the stairs, her hands clasped tightly in front of her. She was aware of Tristan behind her. She could feel the warmth of his body, could hear the sound of his boots on the steps. But she didn't address him. Not until they reached the front door.

She turned to face him then but couldn't bring herself to lift her gaze any higher than the top button of his waistcoat. "I bid you good day, my lord. And I wish you good fortune in all of your business endeavors."

"Miss March…"

"Please don't. Lady Hermione is right. There's no need for us to remain betrothed. And if you'd only…"

Her words disappeared in a tremulous breath at the feel of his fingers touching her beneath her chin. He gently raised her face until she was forced to look him in the eye. "Have you lost faith in me?"

She swallowed hard. "No, my lord." It was the truth. He would marry her. He would keep his word if she let him. "I believe you'll do the honorable thing. And so must I."

Dawning realization registered on Tristan's face. "Valentine—"

"Goodbye, Lord St. Ashton," she said. "I release you from our engagement."

Chapter Fourteen

Kent, England
Autumn, 1861

With every miserable mile of railway track they covered during their journey from London to Caddington Park in Kent, Valentine became more and more convinced that she had no one but herself to blame. If she'd been less scrupulous, she would have held Tristan to his promise. She would have insisted he marry her, even if he didn't want her. Even if he didn't love her. But she couldn't do it. She would as soon keep a wild animal in a cage or try to turn a wolf into a lapdog.

Knowing that, it shouldn't matter that Tristan had readily acceded to the termination of their engagement. It shouldn't break her heart that he'd gone without putting up the slightest argument.

It was a very good thing, she reflected as she settled deeper into her seat, that she hadn't acted in the hope of forcing a declaration from him. If so, she would have been sorely disappointed. He hadn't uttered one word of affection. He hadn't even touched her except to grasp her by the chin and force her to look at him.

She sighed. It was all quite unromantic. And he the biggest rake and reprobate of them all. Clearly there was something wrong with her. The only time he'd ever spoken or behaved in a passionate manner was that night in the conservatory. He'd said it had nothing to do with drink, but how could she believe it when he'd behaved with so much restraint afterward?

"We're approaching the station," Lady Hermione said.

Lord Lynden was seated beside her. He was wearing a heavy topcoat and held a carved ebony cane in his gloved hands. It was the first week of December and the cold weather had come in icy and damp. "We may yet have a white Christmas," he had remarked earlier.

Mundane comments about the weather had been the limit of their conversation for the past forty miles at least. Valentine didn't think any of them were particularly keen on visiting Caddington Park. The outcome was practically guaranteed to be a grim one.

But there was no avoiding it, especially now that Lady Brightwell and her daughter had arrived in town. If they shared the story of Valentine's indiscretion in Yorkshire, the news would swiftly circulate through society and, inevitably, make its way to Caddington Park. And if the Marquess of

Stokedale were to hear of it, his prejudice against her would be insurmountable.

"I will see to hiring the carriage," Lord Lynden said.

"Nonsense," Lady Hermione objected. "I didn't invite you to accompany us so that we might hang on your sleeve, sir. We shall pay our own way."

Lord Lynden glanced out the window. The train was slowing, the wooden platform at Bolton Heath Station rising up on either side of it. "You didn't invite me at all, if you'll recall."

"I sent my footman round with a note."

"Hardly an invitation, madam, but I'll not argue with you."

The train came to a halt in a grinding screech of metal. Valentine smoothed the folds of her cloak. Beneath it, she wore the same brown woolen travelling dress she'd worn on the journey to meet Lady Hermione. She'd paired it with tan gloves of buttery soft kid, half-boots of polished morocco, and a low-brimmed spoon bonnet with wide silk ribbons knotted beneath her chin. Even her hair had been given special attention. She'd brushed it to a high gloss and then rolled it back into an oversized chignon at the nape of her neck. The whole was secured with dozens of pins, many of which were poking and pulling at her scalp.

She wouldn't be at all surprised if she ended this day with a blinding headache. And it would serve her right for trying to impress a man who had treated her so shabbily.

"Miss March," Lady Hermione said abruptly. "You're looking peaked. You're not going to be ill, are you?"

"No, ma'am," Valentine said.

Lord Lynden stood. "Come. We'll all feel better in the fresh air."

Valentine trailed behind Lord Lynden and Lady Hermione as they disembarked. The railway platform was deserted. They were obliged to wait a quarter of an hour for the stationmaster's boy to fetch a carriage and driver to take them to Caddington Park.

True to his word, Lord Lynden arranged all—a fact which seemed to rankle Lady Hermione to no small degree.

"We could have managed just as easily on our own," she grumbled as Lord Lynden handed her up into the carriage. "Women are not helpless, you know. Though I daresay St. Ashton must think so. It was he who insisted you accompany us."

Lord Lynden assisted Valentine into the carriage and then climbed in himself, taking the seat across from her and Lady Hermione. "I'm aware," he said. "He's explained his reasoning to me and I can find no fault with it."

"You spoke to him?" Valentine asked.

"I dined with him last night at my club," Lord Lynden said.

And then he said no more. Valentine ached to question him, but her pride wouldn't allow it. She'd ended her engagement to Tristan. She had no more rights over him. No more reason to enquire after his whereabouts and his welfare.

"He believes Stokedale will accord us more respect if we arrive with a man." Lady Hermione wrapped her mantle more snugly around her shoulders. "Perhaps he's right. Stokedale's opinions on women's issues are sorely outdated. I pity his wife and daughters."

Valentine looked at Lady Hermione in alarm. "They won't be in residence, will they?"

"No, no." Lady Hermione waved the question away with a flick of her hand. "They're on the continent. The family won't come together until Christmas."

The words *family* and *Christmas* triggered a pang of melancholy in Valentine's already heavy heart. This would be her first Christmas without her father. She supposed she would spend it with Lady Hermione, but the future hadn't been discussed as yet.

She'd only come there to stay for the period of her engagement. In a year's time, she was to marry Tristan and go to Northumberland. But now that she was no longer engaged, there was really no need to remain with one of her relations. She would have to start planning for the rest of her life. Whether that life be in India, China, or back in Hartwood Green with Mrs. Pilcher.

Unfortunately, since Tristan's departure yesterday, she found that the idea of missionary work in an exotic land—an idea which had once filled her with earnest enthusiasm—was no longer as exciting as in months gone by. She could summon no interest in travelling to a foreign country or learning a foreign language. She felt lost. Unmoored.

"Ah," Lord Lynden said. "There is Caddington Park."

Valentine leaned to look out the window. She could make out an enormous structure of cold, gray stone. It was built in the Palladian style, all graceful lines and muted dignity. She pressed a hand to her midsection. Her stomach was churning. She'd been too nervous to eat any breakfast. And she very much feared she'd laced her corset too tightly.

"A handsome prospect, isn't it?" Lady Hermione said.

She nodded. "Very handsome."

The carriage stopped at the wide stone steps that led to the front doors. As they disembarked, they were met by a silver-haired butler and two footmen in livery. The butler recognized Lady Hermione at once. He even appeared to know Lord Lynden.

"My lord, my lady," he said. And then his eyes found Valentine. He visibly started.

"I know what you're thinking, Frith," Lady Hermione said briskly. "And you're not wrong. It's why we've come. Do inform Stokedale, won't you? And set us in front of a fire. We are frozen through."

"Yes, my lady," the butler said.

He ushered them through a grand hall and into a small salon. It was simply furnished with sofas, chairs, and several inlaid tables. Heavy oil paintings decorated the brocade-covered walls, and the floor was covered with a thick Oriental carpet. A fire was blazing in the hearth. Lady Hermione went to stand in front of it, her hands extended toward the flames.

Valentine didn't know what to do with herself. Upon entering, she'd given her cloak, bonnet, and gloves to a footman. Rather nonsensically, she wished she could have them back again. She felt vulnerable and exposed without them.

"Courage," Lord Lynden murmured.

She gave him a weak smile.

They were not obliged to wait long. In less than a quarter of an hour, the door to the salon opened and a gentleman entered the room.

He was of medium height and build with hair the color of golden wheat and eyes a cool shade of slate gray. He had sculpted features with a decisive chin and a straight, uncompromising nose. His posture, too, was straight and unbending—inflexible and decidedly unfriendly. He was dressed for the country in tweed trousers and a loose-fitting coat.

"Hermione," he said. "Lord Lynden. This is an unexpected surprise."

"Stokedale." Lady Hermione moved from the fireplace and beckoned for Valentine to come stand beside her. "Allow me to present Miss Valentine March, formerly of Surrey."

Lord Stokedale's gray eyes came to rest on her face. He regarded her for a long while, his brows drawn and his lips pressed into a thin, disapproving line.

Valentine's palms grew damp and her mouth went dry. She felt the weight of Lady Hermione's hand upon her back. She couldn't tell if it was to lend her support or to prevent her from running away.

"You're Sara's daughter," he said finally.

"Yes, my lord."

"You want money, I suppose."

She stiffened. "Indeed I do not, sir."

"Didn't you write to me? Requesting assistance of some sort? My secretary, I assume, has disposed of the letters, but if memory serves—"

"I wrote to you because my father had died. I had no family left. No one to whom I could turn for help."

"And you thought to come here, did you?" Lord Stokedale sighed. "Hermione, this is beyond the pale, even for you."

"Won't you recognize her?" Lady Hermione demanded. "Won't you try to make amends for what happened to Sara?"

"I'm not the one who ordered Sara out of the house," Lord Stokedale said. "I was at Oxford. There's nothing I could have done." He cast another narrow glance at Valentine. Distaste registered in his face. "We don't even know who her father is."

"My father," Valentine said, "was Peregrine March, the late Vicar of Hartwood Green in Surrey. He married my mother in November of 1834, three months before I was born. He came to her aid when her family wouldn't. She might have died otherwise, and I along with her."

"Yet she did die," Lord Stokedale said.

"Yes, she…" Valentine faltered. "She died bringing me into this world. I never knew her, but I would have liked to have known her family. *My* family."

Lord Stokedale strolled to the opposite end of the room. He stopped in front of a portrait of an eighteenth century gentleman in a powdered wig posed with his hunting dogs. "I find this discussion to be in extraordinarily bad taste. My sister's behavior is not the sort of family history one discusses with strangers. However, since you have broached the subject, I will speak plainly. It's not common practice in polite society to recognize children born on the wrong side of the blanket."

"She's Sara's daughter," Lady Hermione said. "Your sister's only child, Stokedale. Don't let your pride—"

"You travelled here by train?" he asked. "You should have telegraphed. I might have saved you the journey."

"You're being damned uncivil," Lord Lynden said.

Lord Stokedale turned to face them. "I am being exceedingly civil. We're an old and honored family, Lynden. A sizeable family. Were we to begin welcoming every bastard and by-blow with a claim on one of our members, we may as well establish an orphanage."

Lady Hermione inhaled a sharp breath. "You go too far, sir."

"It's you who have gone too far, madam," Lord Stokedale said. "Sara has been dead more than a quarter of a century and there are still those who speak of her disgrace. What you've done will only serve to fan the flames of a scandal that's never fully died. You should never have brought her here. Even a woman as reckless as you can't fail to appreciate the consequences of such a rash act."

"And how do you propose to behave when you encounter her out in society?" Lord Lynden asked.

"A remote prospect," Lord Stokedale said. "We're unlikely to move in the same circles."

"It won't be unlikely," Lord Lynden retorted. "It will be inevitable. Miss March is betrothed to my heir. She will soon be the Viscountess St. Ashton."

"Betrothed to your heir?" Lord Stokedale managed to look both intrigued and appalled. "You can't be serious."

A flicker of guilt pinged at Valentine's conscience. She knew full well that she should object. She should explain that, as of yesterday, she and Tristan were no longer engaged. She'd meant to confess it to Lady Hermione directly it happened, but the timing hadn't seemed right. Not with their impending journey to Caddington Park weighing so heavily on all of their minds. And now…

The timing was even less auspicious than yesterday.

No, there would be no confessions in the presence of Lord Stokedale. She would have to bite her tongue and hope that later, in the carriage, when she finally admitted the truth, Lord Lynden and Lady Hermione wouldn't be too angry with her.

"I'm deadly serious," Lord Lynden said. "If you treat my future daughter-in-law with disrespect, the rest of society will think they've been given carte blanche to do the same. And that's something my son will not tolerate. It's something *I* will not tolerate." He gave Lord Stokedale a hard look. "You speak of great families and noble bloodlines. The first Earl of Lynden fought at the side of King Richard the Lionheart. We count ourselves one of the oldest and most distinguished families in England. A fact which you as good as acknowledged when, some years past, you suggested a match between my heir and one of your own daughters."

Lord Stokedale's cold expression betrayed a flash of heat. "I'll thank you not to discuss my daughters," he said tightly. "And you're correct, sir. The conversation you allude to *was* some years past. When our children were still in the nursery.

Well before St. Ashton had acquired his current reputation, I might add."

Lord Stokedale walked to another of his paintings. He gave every sign that he was contemplating the handsome piece of artwork. But his creased brow and rigid posture told another story. He was furious.

"What is it exactly that you would have me do?" He enquired at last. "Acknowledge her on the street? Nod to her in passing? Or do you require something more? A notice in the papers, perhaps."

"Must you be so snide about the matter, Stokedale?" Lady Hermione said.

"If you expect me to rejoice at the connection, madam—"

"I expect no such thing."

"Her father might have been a footman," Lord Stokedale railed. "A groom in my father's stable. One of the groundskeeper's boys."

At that moment, the door opened and Lord Stokedale's butler entered. He cleared his throat. "I beg your pardon, my lord."

Lord Stokedale frowned. "What is it, Frith?"

"His lordship the Viscount St. Ashton has arrived. Shall I—"

He was interrupted by a deep and all too familiar voice. "There's no need to announce me, Frith. We are all of us well acquainted."

Valentine's eyes widened as Tristan walked into the room. He was clad in travelling clothes. A handsome wool overcoat worn over a black frock coat and trousers. He looked as if he'd just climbed down from a carriage or disembarked from the train. Slightly dusty and a little rumpled. She watched, speechless, as he stripped off his gloves and his tall hat and handed them to the butler.

"St. Ashton," Lady Hermione breathed. "Of all the—"

"Madam," Tristan said. "My lords." His eyes found hers. "Miss March."

"What are you doing here?" she asked.

"I have come for you," he said.

"To lend your support?" Lord Lynden frowned deeply. "You're a little late, sir."

Tristan glanced at his father. "It couldn't be helped. I've been in Westminster this morning. I was briefly detained at the home of a charming widow."

Lady Hermione stifled a groan. "Really, my lord."

Tristan continued, unperturbed. "She was telling me about her late son. A young man who perished during the burning of parliament in 1834."

Lord Lynden gave his son an arrested look.

"Only one man perished in that blaze," Stokedale interjected in irritation. "That young secretary of Lord Worthington's. Rutherford somebody or other."

"Val Rutherford," Lord Lynden murmured.

Lady Hermione's eyes shot to his. "Val, did you say?"

But Tristan didn't seem to notice his father. Or anyone else in the room. He held Valentine's gaze. "Your father wasn't a vicar, I'm afraid," he said. "Nor was he a footman or a groom or a groundskeeper's assistant. He was a gentleman. Some might even call him a hero."

Chapter Fifteen

The color drained from Valentine's face, turning her porcelain skin to alabaster. "I don't understand."

Tristan was at her side in an instant. He rested a hand on the small of her back and guided her to a nearby settee. "Sit down and I shall explain."

Once he had her established on the settee, he sank down beside her. Her skirts bunched around his legs in a profusion of brown wool and starched petticoats. He was aware he was too close, but he made no effort to set himself at a distance. How could he think of propriety when she was looking so lost and vulnerable and utterly dear? When the faintest scent of her perfume sent his senses reeling?

Orange blossoms. A sweet, feminine fragrance that turned his brain to mush and caused his heart to thud heavily in his chest.

He wished to God his father, Stokedale, and Lady Hermione would see fit to leave. But they showed no interest in going. They were each watching with avid attention. Each waiting for him to tell them what the devil it was he was talking about.

"The illustrations in your book of Bible verses," he said. "In Yorkshire they were covered with ink. I never saw them properly until yesterday. When I did, I recognized them. At least, I recognized the drawing you recreated on the frontispiece."

"The stag and the lion," Valentine said.

Tristan nodded. "It's from a coat of arms. Initially I didn't know which, but a visit to my club soon answered the question. It belongs to the Baronage of Rutherford." He paused, worried he was overwhelming her. But there was nothing for it. She needed to know. And, if the scraps of conversation he'd overheard before entering the room were any indication, so, too, did Lord Stokedale. "The late Baron Rutherford had three sons," he said. "The youngest was secretary to George Fortescue, Earl of Worthington."

"Rutherford's youngest son," Lord Stokedale repeated. "By God, now I remember. He accompanied Worthington here in the spring of '34. And then again that summer. Worthington and my father were consulting over some political matter. Something to do with the poor laws."

"Val Rutherford," Lady Hermione said. "Astonishing."

"Valentine Rutherford," Tristan corrected. He gave Valentine a fleeting, private smile. "I told you I had never before met a woman named Valentine."

"I thought I was named after a saint," she said. "It's what Papa always told me."

"You were named after your father," Tristan said. "Your natural father. The man who Lady Sara Caddington went to meet at that inn in Surrey. The man in whose memory she sketched all those stags and lions and wrote all those mournful, romantic Bible verses."

"He never came."

"He couldn't. He died when the fire broke out. His mother tells me he was attempting to rescue two servants who were trapped in an interior room. He managed to save them in the end."

"At the cost of his own life," Lord Lynden said. "I remember the incident. It was in all the papers."

Tristan couldn't remember it himself. He'd been too young. Just a child, really. And all he had learned in the years that followed was that the Palace of Westminster had been largely destroyed in the conflagration. He'd had no knowledge of the people affected by the blaze—and certainly not of the twenty-year-old man who'd perished.

"Do you suppose she read it in the papers?" Valentine asked him softly. "And that was why she was sitting in the church and weeping?"

He took one of her hands in his. It was small and slim and cold as ice. He held it gently in his much larger grasp. "I suspect so."

"You said she was too proud to go home."

"I believe her heart was broken," he said. "And that whatever her father said to her was unforgiveable."

"It was," Lord Stokedale said abruptly. For a weighted moment it seemed as if he would say no more. And then he spoke again, his tone brusque. "He told her he wouldn't accept her child. That she must consent to send it away. She refused. At the time I thought…" One fist clenched at his side. "I thought it was merely her damned pride. But if she loved Rutherford, and if he'd died in such a way…"

"She would never have given up her child," Lady Hermione said. "Not for worlds. Not our Sara."

Tristan looked at Valentine's pale face. "Does it help to know the truth?"

Her brows knit. "Yes, but…"

"But?"

"This lady you saw in Westminster…"

"Your grandmother."

"Does she know about me?"

"I didn't tell her," he said. "That must be your decision. But if you decide you'd like to meet her, I don't think she'd turn you away."

Valentine's fingers curled around his. "You visited her this morning. And you discovered all of this…" She searched his face. "I still don't understand why you did it. After what I said to you yesterday—"

"I'll tell you why," he interrupted. "But not here. We will talk in the carriage."

She blinked. "What carriage?"

"The one I have waiting in the drive." He heard Lady Hermione make a sound of dismay, but he ignored her. He hadn't come this far to be thwarted by an overprotective Caddington relation. "Shall we take our leave?"

Valentine cast an anxious glance to Lord Lynden and Lady Hermione.

"Never mind them," Tristan told her. "Come. The horses will be getting restless. I didn't plan to linger." He stood and, much to his relief, she allowed him to pull her to her feet.

"St. Ashton," Lady Hermione said. "This is beyond anything."

"Let them go, ma'am," Lord Lynden said. "Miss March has had enough for today."

Tristan met his father's eyes. For the first time in his life, he saw no judgment or condemnation in his sire's gaze. Instead, much to his amazement, he saw understanding. Perhaps even a little pride.

He inclined his head. "Sir."

"St. Ashton," Lord Lynden said. "Miss March. Mind how you go."

Tristan led Valentine to the door. It opened ahead of them, as if by magic. How many servants had been huddled outside listening? But it was only Frith who stood on the other side of the door. The old butler looked at Valentine, his eyes suspiciously bright.

"Ma'am," he said as he handed her her bonnet, gloves, and cloak. "If I may be so bold…you look very like your mother."

"That will be all, Frith," Lord Stokedale said sharply. And then, "St. Ashton? Miss March? I would have a word, if you please."

Tristan's jaw tightened at Stokedale's approach. Had circumstances been different, he would have given the fellow the same treatment he'd meted out to Phillip Edgecombe.

But one could hardly throw a marquess out of his own ancestral home and into the gutter, no matter how much he might deserve it.

"I'll do as Hermione asks," Lord Stokedale said. "In memory of my sister, I'll acknowledge you in public, Miss March. I'll instruct my family to treat you with all civility. I trust that will be sufficient."

Tristan felt Valentine tuck her hand more firmly in his arm. She was trembling, fine shivers that coursed through her small frame like electric shocks.

And, in that moment, he could have happily murdered the Marquess of Stokedale.

Civility? What in blazes! She'd come all this way, looking for the smallest scrap of familial affection, and Stokedale offered her civility? It was all he could do to keep himself from throttling the pompous ass.

Valentine, by contrast, remained outwardly composed. Despite her tremors, her voice was steady. "I thank you for your condescension, sir. But I don't think we'll have cause to meet again."

Tristan fancied he could see a flicker of relief in Stokedale's eyes. He didn't remain long enough to be certain. After taking his leave of his father and Lady Hermione, he led Valentine out the door. The butler escorted them through the hall and down the front steps to the carriage Tristan had hired in the nearby village of Bolton Heath. It was a newer vehicle, well sprung and comfortably fitted out. He handed Valentine up into it and then climbed in to sit beside her. The coachman shut the door behind them. Seconds later, the horses had been given the office to start and the carriage lumbered into motion.

"Are we going to the station?" Valentine asked.

Tristan's pulse thrummed. He was nervous and damnably uncertain. It was a bloody uncomfortable feeling. "No," he said at last. "We are not."

"Then where…?"

"I don't know, Miss March," he answered. "And that's the problem. Where we go next is not up to me. It's entirely up to you."

Valentine had never seen Tristan look so unsure. Not since the night he'd kissed her in the conservatory. But this was different, somehow. He wasn't melancholy. And he certainly hadn't been drinking.

He cleared his throat. "But before you decide our destination, answer me this. Yesterday…in London…"

"Yes?"

A muscle worked in his jaw. "Why did you release me from our engagement?"

It wasn't the question she'd expected. Indeed, she'd thought he would ask something about her mother or the Caddingtons or even Val Rutherford, the man she now understood to be her natural father. The breaking of their engagement, an incident which, at the time, had seemed to affect him so little, could hardly be of concern to him now, could it?

"There was no need for us to remain engaged," she said. "Not when I'm settled with Lady Hermione and you're making such a success of things in Northumberland. Neither of us particularly needs the other anymore, do we? My reputation is safe. And you needn't fear being cut off from your father's money. There's no longer any purpose—"

"Is that how you feel?" he demanded.

She looked away from him. Her fingers plucked nervously at one of her gloves. "I'd never forgive myself if I let you act out of obligation. And you'd never forgive me either. In time, you may even come to hate me for allowing you to make such a sacrifice."

"A sacrifice," he repeated. "Is that what you think? That I would sacrifice myself in marriage because I've compromised you?"

"I know that you would."

"With my reputation?" he scoffed. "Any number of people have warned you about me. If you think I'd behave in such a noble fashion, you clearly haven't been listening to them."

"I know what your reputation was before, my lord. But you were at a crossroads the day I met you. You have ever since tried to do the right and honorable thing. Even if it made you uncomfortable. It's why you went to Northumberland."

He regarded her for a long moment, an expression in his eyes hard to read. "What of your heart, Miss March? In Yorkshire you said it was mine."

A deep, mortified blush rose in Valentine's cheeks. She wished she'd never said it. But there was no taking it back. Not now. It was the truth, after all. "So it is."

"And what about my heart?"

"*Your* heart?" Her brows lifted in surprise. "That's never been a concern, surely."

"The hell it hasn't," he growled. "Why the devil do you think I've done all of this? Attempting to become independent. Tracking down the origins of your real father. Staying away from you when I might have written or visited or—"

"Because it was the right thing to do. The *honorable* thing to do."

"Curse the honorable thing," he said. "I did it because I'm in love with you."

Valentine's mouth fell open. She felt, for one frozen second, as if he'd spoken to her in Ancient Greek or Swahili. The words were so foreign. So shockingly unexpected. She could only reckon that she'd misheard them. "What did you say?" she whispered.

Tristan looked down at her, a vulnerability in his gaze that she'd never seen before. "I said that I'm in love with you. And I've come to Kent with this blasted carriage and four to ask you to come away with me, my fair one. To Gretna Green. To India, or China, or St. George's Hanover Square. To anywhere you please." He brought his hand to her cheek. It was large and warm, cradling her face like a delicate treasure. "I've come to ask you to marry me, Valentine. Not because I compromised you. Not because of my father's money or because I must do the honorable thing, but because I love you. More than I've ever loved anyone or anything in this world."

She blinked rapidly against a sudden swell of tears. "Do you?"

"Yes, you little fool." His deep voice made the words a caress. "I've loved you since the moment I saw you in the folly. Since you quoted that Bible verse at me. It was the most damnable thing. But you were right. The winter was over the day I met you."

"Oh, Tristan," she said. "This is…" Her voice broke. "This is all quite unexpected."

The pad of his thumb brushed along the delicate bones of her cheek with infinite tenderness, wiping away the first spill of tears. And then, with a muttered oath, he took her in his arms and kissed her.

Valentine wrapped her arms around his neck and clung to him as his lips moved on hers. He wasn't gentle. Nor was he careful. He employed none of his rakish arts. He kissed her as if he were a starving man, made insensible from want. As if she were as essential to him as light and air.

"Obligation," he muttered when they paused for breath. "Is that what you thought I felt for you?" He pressed a kiss to her cheek as he held her. "You mad, beautiful creature. How little you know of men."

Her fingers twined through the thick black hair at the nape of his neck. Her bosom was pressed tight to his chest. She could feel his heart hammering against her own. "I wanted to believe you cared for me," she said softly. "But I dared not hope."

"If I cared for you any more, I would be a candidate for bedlam."

"You never said anything."

"No." His expression sobered. "My words haven't ever counted for much with women. They came too easily. All the compliments, flattery, and broken promises. I wanted to give you something better. Deeds, not words. I wanted to show you that your faith in me wasn't misplaced."

"Of course it wasn't. I knew that. I've always known that. Still..." Her lips tilted briefly in a rueful half-smile. "I wish you'd shown your feelings on occasion. It would've saved me many a sleepless night."

"I would if I hadn't stayed away. There would have been no hiding it. And then the whole world would have known."

"Known what?"

"That I love you. That I adore you beyond reason."

She felt his hands move on her back. He squeezed her corseted waist and brushed kisses over her tightly pinned hair. He couldn't seem to stop touching her. "That's not truly why you did all of those things, is it?" she asked. "Going to Northumberland and trying to be responsible. It wasn't all for me, was it?"

"In the beginning," he admitted. "But as time passed... Good God, Valentine, you wouldn't believe it, but I actually *like* the Priory. If you discount the mud and the weather and the lack of society—"

"You were born to run a great estate," she said. "It's what you've been raised for all your life."

"Yes, but I never thought I would enjoy it. I never once believed it could make me happy."

"Has it?"

"It has," he said. "As much as I could be happy without you by my side. That I kept away from you a month is nothing short of a miracle."

Her eyes welled up. "When you didn't come with us on the journey from Yorkshire, I feared I would never see you again."

"Foolish of you."

"Yes, it was rather, when I always knew that you would keep your promise."

Tristan found her mouth again in a swift, hard kiss before drawing back to look at her tearstained face. "Still weeping, are we?"

"A little."

"I trust they are tears of happiness."

She gave a choked laugh and brought her hands to her face to wipe her cheeks. "They must be," she said. "For I'm so dreadfully happy."

"You're forever without a handkerchief, Miss March. It's a good thing I'm here to look after you." Tristan released her just long enough to retrieve a clean, square of linen from an interior pocket of his coat. He pressed it into her hand. "Come now. Dry your eyes and say that you'll marry me. Say that you love me just a little."

Valentine dabbed at her face with his handkerchief. "Haven't I said so?"

"No," he said grimly. "You most certainly have not."

She met his eyes. The raw emotion she saw there made her heart turn over. "Of course I love you. And more than just a little."

Tristan's gaze held hers. "How much more?"

"So much more that, when you left Lady Hermione's yesterday, I thought my heart would break into a million pieces. And now that you're here, I think you must marry me straightaway, Tristan. For I never want to be apart from you again for as long as I live. No matter how much you might vex me."

He bent his head and pressed a soft, lingering kiss to her temple. "To the train station, then. And on to Gretna Green."

She nodded. "Yes, please."

"And after that?" he asked. "Where shall we go? London? Northumberland? On a mission to some foreign land?"

"Anywhere," she told him. "Everywhere. All of those places. It doesn't matter as long as I'm with you."

Tristan settled her in his arms. "My own precious love. The feeling is entirely mutual."

Epilogue

Tristan Sinclair, Viscount St. Ashton married Valentine March at Gretna Green, Scotland on the sixth of December 1861. The newly wed couple honeymooned at Blackburn Priory, their estate in Northumberland, before travelling to Sinclair House in Devonshire for the Christmas Holidays.

Their scandalous union was the subject of the gossip columns for well over a year, with many speculating that the notorious viscount had ruined the equally notorious daughter of the late Lady Sara Caddington and been forced into marriage by his disapproving father, the Earl of Lynden. In time, however, it became clear to all that St. Ashton was deeply and irrevocably in love with his wife and she with him. This was never more apparent than when, in their second year of marriage, Lord St. Ashton accompanied his wife on a lengthy tour of the British missions in India.

Lord and Lady St. Ashton would go on to welcome their first child in 1863. They christened her Sara Eleonore Sinclair, after their respective mothers.

The End

Acknowledgments

As always, I owe tremendous thanks to those who helped to polish the final manuscript of *The Viscount and the Vicar's Daughter* into the story that it is today.

To my wonderful British and American beta readers, Sarah and Flora, thank you for your time, your generosity, and all of your helpful feedback. I am so grateful to have you both in my corner.

To my fantastic editor, Deb Nemeth, thank you for all of your kind comments and suggestions. Your scrupulous attention to detail—both grammatical and historical—has made this a stronger book (and me a better writer).

To my amazing publicist, Emma Boyer at Smith Publicity, thank you for your tireless efforts on my behalf. I'm so happy to have a fellow Victorian era (and dressage!) enthusiast to promote my fiction projects.

To my fabulous friends, fans, and followers across social media and print, thank you for your readership. Your kind comments, messages, and reviews make all the hard work worthwhile.

And, finally, to my parents, Vickie and Eugene, thank you for supporting and encouraging my writing—even when it's a project I don't let you read.

About the Author

Mimi Matthews writes both historical non-fiction and traditional historical romances set in Victorian England. Her articles on nineteenth century social history have been published on various academic and history sites, including the Victorian Web and the Journal of Victorian Culture, and are also syndicated weekly at BUST Magazine. In her other life, Mimi is an attorney with both a Juris Doctor and a Bachelor of Arts in English Literature. She resides in California with her family, which includes an Andalusian dressage horse, two Shelties, and two Siamese cats.

To learn more, please visit
www.MimiMatthews.com

Other Titles by Mimi Matthews

NON-FICTION

The Pug Who Bit Napoleon:
Animal Tales of the 18th and 19th Centuries

A Victorian Lady's Guide to Fashion and Beauty
Coming in July 2018 from Pen and Sword Books

FICTION

The Lost Letter
A Victorian Romance

The Advertisement
A Victorian Romance
Coming in April 2018 from Perfectly Proper Press

CPSIA information can be obtained
at www.ICGtesting.com
Printed in the USA
LVOW12s1629270218
568056LV00001B/39/P